"Rachel, earlier tonight, someone broke into greenhouse four."

"Greenhouse four? *My* greenhouse?" Technically, it was *his* greenhouse, but the only things in it were her Malaysian basil plants. "Were you there? Are you okay?"

Edward paused, and his searching gaze made her stomach flip. "I'm fine. I wasn't there when it happened. I left my cell phone in greenhouse six, so I went to get it. I noticed movement in the yard, and when I went to check the greenhouses, I found yours unlocked. Someone trashed all your plants."

She gasped. She needed Edward to cultivate a certain number of plants so she could make the extract for her scar reduction cream, scheduled to launch in only five months. She couldn't be late. The spa depended on her new product launch. "Why didn't the alarm go off? I thought the greenhouses all had security alarms in place."

"They do," Edward said. "But the system in greenhouse four didn't go off. I checked it, and it looks like the thief tampered with it. Whoever did this was a professional, not your average thief. The thief entered only greenhouse four, Rachel—the thief was only after *your* plants."

Books by Camy Tang

Love Inspired Suspense

Deadly Intent
Formula for Danger

CAMY TANG

writes romance with a kick of wasabi. Originally from Hawaii, she worked as a biologist for nine years, but now she writes full-time. She is a staff worker for her San Jose church youth group and leads a worship team for Sunday service. She also runs the Story Sensei fiction critique service, which specializes in book doctoring. On her blog, she gives away Christian novels every Monday and Thursday, and she ponders frivolous things like dumb dogs (namely, hers), coffee-geek husbands (no resemblance to her own…), the writing journey, Asiana and anything else that comes to mind. Visit her Web site at www.camytang.com.

FORMULA FOR DANGER

CAMY TANG

Steeple
Hill®

Published by Steeple Hill Books™

STEEPLE HILL BOOKS

**Steeple
Hill®**

Recycling programs
for this product may
not exist in your area.

ISBN-13: 978-0-373-67430-5

FORMULA FOR DANGER

Copyright © 2010 by Camy Tang

www.SteepleHill.com

Printed in U.S.A.

The earth is the Lord's, and everything in it,
the world, and all who live in it.
—*Psalms* 24:1

To Danica and Cheryl. I thought I could never find two people as sick and twisted as myself, but I have in you two. Thanks for being my friends.

ONE

Dr. Rachel Grant had walked only a few feet out the back door of her family's Sonoma day spa, Joy Luck Life, when the patter of running footsteps behind her made her turn.

She had only a glimpse of a dark hoodie and a tall, lanky figure before a shove sent her sprawling onto the sidewalk. *Thwack!* Her left cheekbone collided with the cement, sending pain lancing through her head.

Snow clouded her vision and she struggled to open her eyes. Her heart pounded in her throat, making it hard for her to breathe. Frantic, she opened her mouth wide but no sound came out.

She glanced up. The backsides of dirty sneakers filled her field of view as they trotted away from her. Then a hand scooped up the bag strap of her sister Naomi's laptop computer, which had flown from Rachel's grip to land on the edge of the pool of light from the parking lot streetlamp. The sneakers hustled away.

Breathe! Rachel forced her wooden lungs to fill

and tried to scream, but only a harsh croak came out. Where were the security guards? They should have seen the attack thanks to the outside video cameras. How long would it take for them to run out here?

Even worse, Naomi would be devastated to lose that laptop, which she'd bought barely five hours ago.

She heard the creak of the spa's back door, then more footsteps. "Rachel! Rach, are you okay?" Naomi fell to her knees beside her, hands on Rachel's shoulders. "I was talking to Martin, and we saw it all on the security camera." Martin, one of the security guards, raced past them, pursuing the stranger and the laptop.

In the distance, a woman's voice screeched, "What are you doing? Don't leave me!" It sounded as if it had come from the front of the spa.

Who was that? What was going on?

Rachel pushed herself up, her cheekbone throbbing as she rose. She squeezed her eyes shut to the wave of pain and paused on her knees, her head bowed.

Naomi put her arm around her. "Where are you hurt?"

"Just my cheek."

Naomi pulled Rachel's hair away from her face to look at her. Rachel had a hard time opening her eyes again as the pain splashed across her forehead, trickling back inside her skull. "How bad is it?"

"You'll have a black eye, that's for sure. We need to get you to the hospital."

"No, I'll have Monica look at it first. If the family

nurse says so, *then* I'll go to the hospital." Just the thought of all the people in a crowded emergency room made Rachel cringe. She only wanted a quiet place to lie down and recover. "I'm sorry about your laptop."

"Forget the laptop, I'm worried about you."

"I only took a fall, nothing worse. But that laptop was new—"

"I can buy a new one. Besides, I'm almost glad it was new because it didn't have anything on it, so the spa didn't lose any sensitive information. That would have been worse." Especially since Naomi still managed the spa while their father recovered from his stroke. Naomi had bought the computer to help her with the spa's accounting.

"We should call the police and report it stolen."

"We should call Dad and Aunt Becca first." Naomi dug her cell phone out of her pocket.

"Call Aunt Becca. Aren't she and Detective Carter out to dinner tonight?" The two of them were dating again after an argument that had kept them apart for a few months. It was almost 10:00 p.m., but they might still be together at a movie.

As Naomi talked to Aunt Becca—who indeed was with Detective Horatio Carter—Rachel managed to sit up, although the evening sky spun around her. She clutched her hands together, trying to stop their shaking. She'd been attacked in the spa parking lot!

Clicking heels made Rachel look up. Gloria Reynolds, one of Naomi's massage clients, tripped toward them. "Dr. Grant, are you all right? Did that man hurt you?"

"Ms. Reynolds, you're still here?" Not the most tactful thing to say, but her headache was making it hard for her to be polite.

"Ms. Reynolds was my last client for tonight," Naomi told Rachel as she ended her call with Aunt Becca.

Gloria flipped her highlighted hair with a manicured hand. "The security guard was walking me to my car when he saw that person running away. Miss Grant," Gloria said to Naomi, "you really should talk to that guard. He ran after the person and left me by myself. Even when I called to him. And it was obvious the other guard was after the man, too, so there was no need for him to give chase."

Naomi smiled politely and responded with amazing courtesy when Rachel knew she must be rolling her eyes inside.

A flash of car headlights made Rachel wince as a vehicle headed down the spa driveway.

Then alarm jolted through her. The spa was closed, and the security guards, running after the thief toward the driveway, would have stopped the car from entering. Were the guards okay?

The car maneuvered into the staff parking lot, then stopped right next to them. A door opened and slammed shut. "Rachel!"

Edward Villa's voice made her heart leap into her

throat, then settle back down in her chest, racing. Edward was here. Suddenly everything seemed okay.

No, she had to stop reacting this way to him. He didn't think of her as anything other than a client.

"Are you all right?"

She smelled him—pine, a hint of the orchids he worked with at his greenhouses and earthy musk—before her eyes registered that he was crouched in front of her, edging out Ms. Reynolds.

"The guards told me what happened when I drove in."

She had been able to keep it together when talking to Naomi, but somehow, his concern for her undermined her control over her emotions, and she steeled her jaw against a sudden onslaught of wild sobbing. Casting herself into his arms would only solidify his cool opinion of her, which he had made abundantly clear a couple months ago.

"Rachel." He reached out for her.

She held up a hand to stop him.

He grasped her hand, engulfing her fingers. His callused fingers rubbed her knuckles. His touch made her head spin.

"I'm fine," she whispered, breathless. She pulled her hand away.

The security guards walked up to them. "I'm sorry, Miss Grant, he got away. He ran up the driveway, and there was a car waiting for him at the end of it. They took off."

"Dr. Grant, are you okay?" the other guard asked, peering at Rachel.

She felt like a bug on display. "I'm fine." She heaved herself to her feet, but it made the blood pound painfully in her head. She swayed.

Edward's arm wrapped around her, making the earth stand still again. It felt good to be held by him. It felt…

Too good. She pulled away from him.

Edward paused a moment, then he bent down and collected her purse, which had dropped and scattered its contents when she fell. As he handed it to her, his eyes were calm, but somehow she could sense a fire burning behind them. As if other emotions ran deeper.

She didn't understand. While they had been working together for the past year on Rachel's new product for the spa, they had gotten closer, and she had felt free to be herself with him. But then, in the past couple months, he had withdrawn from her, become distant and polite.

Maybe he had seen who she really was…and he hadn't liked what he saw.

The thought was like a punch to her gut, every time she thought it. Which had been often in the past two months.

No, maybe he had never been interested in her, and he'd suddenly become aware that he was leading her on. Regardless, recently he had been clear in showing that he had no interest in her beyond a good business relationship.

She was just imagining the emotion in his eyes was deeper than natural concern. "Thank you." She took her purse from him, avoiding touching his hand again.

The silence was thicker than cold cream.

"Rachel—" he began.

"Here you go, Miss Rachel." Martin, a security guard who had been with them for years, handed her an ice pack he must have gotten from inside the spa. "That'll keep the swelling down from that shiner."

His light words made her smile, made the situation not seem so horribly violating. "Thanks, Martin." She pressed the cold pack to her eye, and found that it enabled her to avoid looking at Edward.

"Ms. Reynolds," Naomi said, "let me escort you back inside. We can wait for the police in one of the lounge rooms."

Rachel stayed outside and watched them reenter the spa. She tried not to remember what had happened, but it came to her in flashes. She shivered. She'd been bullied in grade school because she'd been a geek and a bit odd, but no one had ever assaulted her. Even bickering with her sisters Naomi and Monica had never gone beyond a little hair-pulling.

But tonight, someone had deliberately *hurt* her. It made her feel weak and vulnerable. Not in control.

And she didn't like it.

She especially didn't like that it had happened here, at the spa.

She suddenly realized that Edward had no reason to visit her here. They usually talked on the phone about the basil plants he was growing for production of her new spa product and met at his greenhouses. Why was he at the spa this late at night? "Edward, what are you doing here?"

His eyes were deep obsidian pools as they studied her, then he surprised her by looking away.

"Edward?"

He sighed. "I called your home and your sister Monica said you were still here."

"Did you try calling my cell phone? Did I not hear it ringing?" She fumbled in her purse and grasped the rubbery edge of her rugged waterproof cell phone—a necessity since she'd ruined two phones by using them while working in the lab with chemicals.

"No, I didn't call."

Avoidance wasn't Edward's style—neither was this vague evasiveness. "Then what…?"

He didn't answer immediately, and his face was grave. "I came to the spa to tell you something you're not going to like."

Her heart beat hard, once. But really, how could her day get any worse? "Lay it on me. I'm ready."

"Earlier tonight, someone broke into greenhouse four."

"Greenhouse four? *My* greenhouse?" Technically, it was *his* greenhouse, but the only things in it were her Malaysian basil plants. "Were you there? Are you okay?"

He paused, and his searching gaze made her stomach flip. But she lifted her head and tightened her muscles to keep her molten insides in place.

"I'm fine. I wasn't there when it happened."

"Oh. Good." She tried to slow her racing heart. "Did you call the police?"

"Yes. I left my brother, Alex, to meet with them while I came to talk to you. On the way, I called Horatio Carter, who said he was also headed here with your aunt, so that was fortunate. I'm hoping he'll come back to the greenhouse with me tonight."

"How did you find out about the break-in?"

"I left my cell phone in greenhouse six, so I went to get it. I noticed movement in the yard, and when I went to check the greenhouses, I found yours unlocked."

Her headache became a jackhammer against her skull. "Was everything okay?"

The lines deepened around his mouth. "No. Someone trashed it—all your plants."

She gasped.

"Don't panic too much. Alex is moving the plants to greenhouse seven right now, and I can salvage most of it."

"Most of it?" She needed Edward to cultivate a certain number of plants so she could make the extract for her scar-reduction cream, scheduled to launch in only five months. She couldn't be late. The spa depended on her new product launch. "Will you be able to grow more? I need..." She faltered at the shadow that crossed his eyes.

He replied evenly, "Your research will be fine, Rachel."

His distant tone confused her. What had she said? She switched tactics. "You left your cell phone in a greenhouse? You never do that. If you hadn't forgotten it..."

A half smile twitched at his mouth. "God was watching over your plants, I think."

The familiar way he said it made something squirm inside her. Edward had always had such a different relationship with God than she did, and it seemed to widen the gap between them. "Why didn't the alarm go off? I thought the greenhouses all had security alarms in place."

"They do—to monitor temperature and humidity, and also to alert when a window or door is opened. But the system in greenhouse four didn't go off. I checked it, and it looks like the thief tampered with it."

"Aren't those security alarms top-of-the-line? High-tech?"

He nodded. "Whoever did this was a professional, not your average thief."

The mild California fall breeze was suddenly frosty against her skin. "How about the other greenhouses?"

"I checked them all. Only yours was broken into."

"Only mine?" This was a blow she didn't know if she could bear, not on top of everything that had happened tonight. She bit her lip.

It almost looked as if he didn't know what to do with his hands, finally resting them on his slim hips. "I don't understand it. Some of the plants in my other greenhouses are extremely rare and valuable, but whoever came by didn't even touch them."

She'd seen those plants—exotic orchids and rare rain-forest species, mostly commissioned by wealthy clients because of Edward's reputation for cultivating delicate tropical plants. "None of them were taken?"

If the burglar could have dismantled the security alarm for one greenhouse, surely he could have dismantled the security alarms for the others. Or maybe he hadn't had time to because Edward had discovered the thief's activities. But why bother with destroying her plants when he could have more quickly gotten into the other greenhouses and stolen the rarer species?

Edward's eyes pinned her with concern and gravity. "The thief entered only greenhouse four, Rach—the thief was only after *your* plants."

Edward hated chaos, and it surrounded him in greenhouse four—broken pots, torn leaves and potting soil dusting everything. He stood in the midst of the destruction and sighed.

It wasn't actually that bad. He'd discovered the open

door before the temperature had dropped too much, and now Rachel's plants were all in greenhouse seven. He was also planning on paying for an evening guard to walk the greenhouses—at least until the person responsible for this was caught.

Detective Carter glanced up from where he surveyed some toppled tables. "It would have been better for me if you'd left the scene as is, Edward."

"Sorry, Detective, but Malaysian basil is extremely sensitive to temperature and humidity. The plants could have died within the hour."

Detective Carter shrugged and went back to taking notes.

"Thanks for convincing Rachel not to come out here tonight, Horatio," Edward said.

The detective shook his head, his thinning red-gold hair glinting dully in the fluorescent light. "She didn't need to see this. She's had a bad night already. How many plants survived?"

"Almost all of them, actually."

Horatio grunted.

"My brother, Alex, and I counted as we transferred the plants. We're only missing about twelve of them, and I'm sure there are a couple lost in the piles of dirt. Some will die later, but we'll try to prevent that."

"I'm about done here." The detective flipped his notebook closed. "You mentioned Alex took pictures of the greenhouse before you two moved the plants?"

Edward nodded. "He's in greenhouse seven right now."

"Good. I wanted to talk to him anyway."

It always amazed Edward how Alex had become such good friends with Detective Carter, who had been the man who had arrested his brother all those years ago for robbing a convenience store.

"I hope not too many plants die because of tonight." Horatio paused as he pulled open the door. "Rachel has been working pretty hard on this new product." He left the greenhouse, heading toward the south side of the property.

Edward's jaw tensed. "Yes," he said softly to himself. He knew exactly how hard she'd been working. At least, how hard she'd started working three months ago. She was probably driving herself into the ground by now.

And why should he care?

He was fooling himself if he thought he didn't care. Seeing her on her knees, her eye swollen and red, had shot him through the heart.

For the past year he had been growing the special Malaysian basil plants she used to create the scar-reduction cream that she planned to launch in a few months. During that year they had grown closer, but a couple of months ago she had discovered how truly revolutionary her product was. She had then thrown herself into her research with single-minded purpose and insanely long hours.

She had spent less time with him, and he had tried

not to let it bother him at first—after all, Rachel's cream, thanks to the Malaysian basil as the secret ingredient, was truly a breakthrough product in reducing scarring, and they were only working together, not dating. But up until that point they had been getting closer, and he had wanted to see if she would take their relationship beyond a professional one. He had asked her to dinner at his mother's house, to meet his family.

She had been pleased and excited, which got his hopes up. But the night of the dinner, thirty minutes late, she had called to say she had found a new formulation and wanted to test it. That she was sorry to have to cancel last minute. Maybe next time?

Mama had been disappointed. For Edward, Rachel's phone call had caused a twist of pain in his gut because it had reminded him of Papa's excuses, the way Papa would cancel last minute, the way Papa would put work before his relationships and all the bitterness and pain coloring Edward's memories of his father.

To protect his heart, he had made a decision to back away from their friendship before it became more than that. He'd thought a couple of months of polite phone conversations and professional meetings here at the greenhouse meant he had distanced himself emotionally.

He'd been deluding himself.

He threw himself into the cleanup work, trying to sweep away the vision of her bruised face. After clearing a path through the dirt and pottery shards on the floor, he righted the tables that had been knocked over, making a mental note to fix the broken leg on one of them.

Snap!

His heart stopped in his chest. The sound had been too loud—like a heavy foot stepping on a branch.

Horatio had left several minutes ago to talk to Alex in greenhouse seven, which was in the opposite direction of where the sound had come from, so it couldn't be either of them. Which meant...

An intruder was outside in the darkness.

He exited the greenhouse as casually as he could, listening for sounds of running footsteps just in case the intruder had seen him leave through the glass of the greenhouse windows and was now escaping. No sounds except a soft rustle of tree leaves in a stray night breeze.

It took too long for his eyes to adjust to the darkness. He moved away from the greenhouse door by feel and smell more than sight, his shoes padding against wet leaves and grass.

The crickets from the pond were loud. He hunkered down near a tree, still and tense.

Suddenly he saw a shadow move.

He circled around, avoiding patches of dry leaves that could give him away, keeping the shadow in sight.

Then the man stopped moving.

Had the figure heard him? Edward froze, trying to

pick the intruder out from the darkness. It was almost impossible—he had to wait until the figure moved again.

Nothing stirred in the darkness for what seemed like hours. His hands started to numb from the cold night air, so he eased them into his pockets to warm them, never taking his eyes from where he'd last seen the intruder. This was private property, and he resented this invasion.

Edward saw a slight movement. The man was short and stocky, or maybe he was hunched down. He almost didn't seem to be trying to stay out of sight. He had stopped under an orange tree, and the overhanging branches partially hid him from sight and protected him—Edward couldn't grab him while the arms of the tree circled him.

Then the man moved.

The stranger eased closer to the greenhouse and seemed to be trying to peer inside. He had to be up to no good. He moved slowly, as stealthy as a coyote.

When the intruder had fully cleared the branches of the orange tree, Edward leaped at him.

They went down in a whirlwind of dead leaves and the stranger's thick jacket. The man was smaller than he had anticipated, but wiry and quick. Edward got a glancing blow to the jaw from a flailing fist that made him jerk back slightly.

The stranger took advantage of the pause to scramble away, or maybe to grab a branch as a weapon. Edward didn't want to find out—he dived for the figure, using all his weight to pin the man to the ground, reaching to capture scrabbling arms and twist them behind the man's back.

"Eep!"

He stilled. Male trespassers didn't *eep*.

He loosened his hold, and the person flipped over.

"Rachel!"

She stilled the moment their eyes met. The light from the greenhouse windows gave her face a pearl-like glow, and he caught a whiff of her perfume— lavender and citrus. She was beautiful, ethereal. The first time she'd come to his greenhouses to hire him, over a year ago, the sight of her had sucked the air out of his lungs. Like now.

No, this was dangerous territory. Edward stood and gave her a hand up.

She busied herself dusting the leaves from her jeans, but at the same time, she seemed to be trying to shrink inside her bulky winter jacket.

"What are you doing, Rachel? Detective Carter said you didn't need to be here."

"Yes, I did." Her eyes, wide, determined, but fighting tears at the same time, met his. "I did. I couldn't stay home and just…" She bit back a sob.

He could understand her need to see for herself the damage done to the plants and how that sight would somehow make her feel more in control of the whole situation. She had been working long hours to develop her scar-reduction cream, and this kind of setback would have thrown her for a loop.

He wanted to hold her, comfort her, tell her it would be all right.

No, he had to keep his distance from her. He and his family had already lived through the broken promises and hurt from a workaholic father. He had vowed he would never neglect his own children for his work, he would never make them feel like a secondary priority in his life, he would never make them feel as if their graduations and work successes were not important enough to attend, as Papa had done to Edward. Therefore, he wouldn't even consider getting involved with a woman who would cause the same sort of pain in her children.

So he'd withdrawn from Rachel. He had to remember why he'd done that.

She shivered, despite her jacket.

"Come inside the greenhouse." He led her into the warm, moist air. The sight was going to upset her, so he watched her closely.

She surprised him. She went completely still as she surveyed the mess. Her bottom lip trembled once. Her hands pressed to her stomach as if to keep herself from falling apart.

Her silence filled the greenhouse, so he spoke tentatively, reiterating what he'd told Detective Carter. "Are you sure you're okay?"

No answer. Her unfocused gaze told him that he'd lost her to her own thoughts.

"Rachel?"

She started, then darted a sideways glance at him. She took a deep breath and adopted a more business-like demeanor. "What do you want me to do?"

"You've had a tough night. Are you sure you want to help clean up? Why not come back tomorrow—"

"No, if I go home, I'll just lie awake worrying about it all." She gave him a small smile. "I'm fine, really. The black eye looks worse than it feels."

Actually, it hadn't colored much yet. It only looked like a trick of the shadows. "Did Monica look at it?"

"She sighed in exasperation and said something like, 'If you insist on gallivanting around Sonoma County with a black eye, don't come crying to me if you faint or get blurry vision. Go to some other nurse, because you won't get sympathy from me.'"

Edward laughed. "Which means, in Monica-speak, that you're okay but she doesn't want to say so." He handed Rachel a broom. "I'll clean up the broken shards. You sweep the dirt into the bin. And look for any plants I might have missed."

They worked in silence for a moment. Then Rachel asked, "Did Detective Carter already leave?"

"No, he's in greenhouse seven. He needed to talk to Alex."

Rachel hesitated a moment before asking, "Is your brother in trouble?"

Edward blinked at her. "No, why?"

"Why would Detective Carter need to talk to him?"

"Oh. Horatio and Alex are friends. Horatio is the officer who arrested Alex for the robbery."

"*The* robbery? The one that sent Alex to prison? That makes no sense."

Edward laughed. "After Alex received Christ in prison, he went straight to Horatio once he got out on parole and thanked him for arresting him. And apologized for giving him so much grief for so many years." He'd have given anything to have witnessed his tall, 220-pound brother apologizing to Detective Carter, who, while steely-eyed and intimidating in his own way, was still five inches shorter than Alex.

"Wow."

"They've become friends in the years since. I think Alex occasionally helps Detective Carter on some of his cases, because of his past experiences and connections he still has."

"Not illegal connections?"

"No, he gave those up. But he still visits several of his old friends asking them to come to church with him."

"Oh." Her eyes skittered away as she renewed her sweeping.

There was only silence for a moment, then Edward said, "Alex said to tell you he was praying for you—"

"Tell him thanks." But her words were curt.

He tried again. "He also said that if you wanted him to pray for anything in particular—"

"No." Her voice was sharp, and she started sweeping

the floor with short, jerky movements. The conversational topic was clearly over.

Strange, she seemed even more uncomfortable talking about her faith now than three months ago, when they had been closer and chatting together more often. They'd rarely discussed God, but she'd never avoided the subject. She had said she was a strong Christian. Was her faith wavering in the face of all the recent problems?

She suddenly stopped and stared at the ground, her broom lax in her hands. He caught the sheen in her eyes, the painful way she pressed her lips shut. Even the red tinge of her nose made his concern well up in him, and before he knew it, he'd crossed the room to gently grasp her shoulders. "Rachel, it's okay."

The smell of her perfume brought it all back to him. He was surrounded by lavender-citrus—the way it melded with her musk made it distinctly *Rachel*. It brought back the memory of dinners spent talking and laughing. The unique way she viewed the world made him think, made him laugh. Being this close to her, he missed that.

She relaxed under his touch, but her head dipped down. He peered over her shoulder at what had caused her distress—a mangled uprooted basil plant, its leaves dark green with damage, the roots tangled into a brown yarn ball. Forlorn and dying.

"Stupid," she whispered. "Crying over a plant."

"It's not just a plant." He knew it was the crux, the

"secret ingredient" of her scar-reduction cream, which made it like gold to her.

He gently lifted his hands from her shoulders and stepped back. "Don't worry. You'll have more than enough basil for the product launch."

"How can you be sure?" Her voice was worrying.

"Because I'm the one raising your plants."

"But you can't guarantee I'll have enough. This product launch is important."

Edward couldn't understand why this launch was everything to her. "Rachel, the world is not going to end if your product launches a month later."

She shook her head. "You never understood the kind of pressure I'm under as the spa's dermatologist." Her shoulders had become stiff again. "You're the good son, the oldest of two brothers, successful and confident."

What? He frowned at her. "What does that have to do with anything?"

"You can't understand what it's like being the oldest of three sisters and yet not as successful as the two of them."

"What do you mean? You are successful. You create innovative products for your father's spa, which has international renown."

She was shaking her head. "In company, my father praises Naomi for her management of the spa while he has been recovering from the stroke. He praises Monica for her nursing helping him recover so quickly.

But he bemoans the fact that my last research project had to be canceled because it wasn't going well. He worries that my last product launched isn't selling as well as he had hoped." She rubbed her forehead.

"Have you talked to him about it?"

"I try, but he just doesn't listen. He doesn't understand me." Her voice cracked.

Her unexpected vulnerability shocked him. Her frailty made him want to wrap her in his arms. In the year they'd been working together on her basil plants and growing closer as friends, she had never been this emotional with him. Then again, she hadn't been suffering under this kind of setback before, either. "I want to understand you, Rachel. If you'd only let me."

She met his eyes, touching him with her gaze like a caress to his cheek. But then her eyes wavered, doubt filling them, stress drawing lines down her face, and she turned away.

He'd lost her.

She turned quickly and grasped a basil plant, shaking it loose from the clumps of dirt on the floor, but holding it so tightly that she bruised its leaves.

Despite the fact that he didn't agree with her workaholic tendencies, they had been more than researcher and gardener. They had been becoming friends. He couldn't deny that this kind of brutal attack on her, leaving her shaken and vulnerable, made him want to help her.

He put his hand over hers, taking the forlorn basil

plant from her fingers. "Don't worry, Rachel. Things will turn out fine."

She shook her head, biting her lip. "I'll never find out who did this."

"Yes, you will. Because I'll help you."

TWO

Rachel's stomach was a block of ice despite the sun warming her back and the sweat dripping down her neck. She pedaled harder, making the wind sting her face as her bike tires ate up the sun-bleached asphalt of the Sonoma country road.

Yesterday had been awful. She couldn't believe that she hadn't been safe in her own spa parking lot. The attack on her plants at Edward's greenhouse felt like an even deeper violation—not just against her, but against her research, against her family's spa.

And last night in the greenhouse, she'd wanted Edward to protect her—to hold her and make everything all right. She'd wanted to unburden herself and wrap herself in his concern.

But she didn't have the right to ask that of him.

Her father had been concerned, but even more than that, he'd been worried about the research, about the product launch. As usual. Unspoken was the specter of her last disastrous venture, and how he'd blamed her for it.

Four years ago she had developed a grape-seed

extract moisturizer for the spa to launch as a new product. A month before Joy Luck Life spa released it, Avignon spa in New York happened to release a grape-seed extract moisturizer, as well. It wasn't the exact formulation, even though it also used a grape-seed extract ingredient, and Rachel hadn't thought it would be a problem to continue with their product launch. Plus, it was too late to stop it. But then Internet news reporters had accused Joy Luck Life of "stealing" Avignon's formula. The spa received a lot of bad press and had been subjected to false rumors, which her father had taken hard, asking her again and again why she had suggested they continue with the product launch.

And now this sabotage of her basil plants, causing a setback for her latest product launch.

She'd considered skipping her daily bike ride this morning, but aside from a low-level headache and some tenderness around her eye, she felt fine. She needed to be alone with her thoughts.

As she neared the base of an upcoming hill, the hum of a car engine came from behind. Her heartbeat sped up for a second as the gleam of chrome seemed to appear directly next to her, blinding her— the vehicle was too close!

Then the auto blazed past her, whipping her in the wind of its wake, making her wobble a bit. She caught a glimpse of the bright sticker of a car-rental company on the bumper before it disappeared over the hill.

Another tourist, viewing the sights of Sonoma

County or maybe getting a *very* early start on a wine-tasting tour. She couldn't complain, since the tourists contributed to the spa's popularity, but their reckless-ness on the roads sometimes made her hug the sides more than normal.

She struggled up the winding hill, the breeze drop-ping with her dwindling speed. The sun warmed her head inside her bike helmet. Her lungs heaved, and she welcomed the exertion, trying to somehow purge her body of all the confusing, frightening feelings of last night.

The greenhouse destruction made it obvious that someone else knew about her research and wanted to stop the product launch. While anyone could have fol-lowed her to the greenhouse at any time, they couldn't know how central those plants were to her current project unless they'd somehow gotten her research notes, which were only on her computer at work.

She couldn't take the chance someone had hacked into her work computer, or could do so in the future. This morning she had called her cousin Jane, a com-puter expert, to ask her if she could come to the spa to upgrade the security on Rachel's work computer and see if someone had breached her system.

Jane was the main reason she had developed the scar-reduction cream, and she could barely repress her desire to present it to her, to feel that she had somehow atoned for what she had done to Jane all those years ago.

When Rachel and her cousin were eight years

old, Rachel had inadvertently started a fire in Jane's playhouse, causing scarring along Jane's cheek and jawbone. Jane said she forgave Rachel, but Rachel couldn't forgive herself. When she'd realized how incredible the results of the cream were, she had doubled her efforts to perfect the formula, thinking of Jane's scars the entire time.

She reached the crest of the hill, her heart pounding. Her entire body was tired today, probably from the stress of last night, getting home so late only to face her father's heavy disapproval, and then rising early to go for a bike ride. Maybe she'd cut her ride short today so she could get into work early. She coasted down the hill, the breeze cooling her, the wind filling her lungs.

Another car engine sounded behind her, ruining the feeling of freedom and being alone out here in the crisp air. She damped down her irritation and, mindful of the last car, moved closer to the side of the road.

The engine seemed abnormally loud—and close. She glanced over her shoulder.

Her movement caused her bike to slip off the asphalt and skid a little in the gravel bordering the road.

Suddenly she felt as if the car behind her had bumped into her back tire. The bike bucked her off and flung her upward.

She screamed.

For a stricken heartbeat she hung poised in midair,

staring at the ground sloping from the road to a field of grapevines. And then she plummeted down, rocks and juniper bushes rising up to meet her.

She curled as she landed, striking her right shoulder with a *crack!* that trembled through her entire frame. She rolled and pitched, head over heels, sideways and underways and every which way. She finally landed with a jarring *thud!* to her spine that snapped her head back into the ground.

For long, excruciating seconds, she couldn't breathe. She couldn't make her diaphragm move. She stared at the pale blue sky, misted with incoming clouds, and struggled to make her body obey her frantic mind.

Then she gasped long and hard. She coughed, hacking up dust from her lungs, burning her throat. And pain exploded in her bones.

She curled onto her side, thorns pricking her cheek. She could suddenly hear the whistle of the wind, and the receding sound of a car engine.

Someone had hit her—and was driving away.

He'd come. The one man she wouldn't have expected but wanted.

As soon as Edward's truck pulled alongside her and she met his fierce gaze through the windshield, she relaxed muscles that she hadn't realized were tight.

She had never been more thankful for her rugged waterproof phone—it had been unscathed from her accident. After calling Aunt Becca, she'd made her way back to the road and moved away from the sloping hill so that she'd be out of range of any cars speeding down. Also, a stubby tree that she could lean against grew a few feet in from the road. She still felt as if her bones were creaking, but at least she could walk.

She vaguely registered Naomi, Monica and Aunt Becca also getting out of the four-door truck, but Edward filled her vision. He reached her first, folding her in his tanned arms, strong and warm, smelling of earth and pine.

He had never embraced her before.

She never wanted to move again.

"Are you all right?"

"Where's your bike?"

"You look awful. Let me look at you."

This last was from Monica, who wedged between them so she could stare critically at Rachel's face and her limbs. "Any pain when you walk?"

"No." She glanced around Monica's head, but Edward had already walked away, his back to her.

Her sister touched her at various places on her body. "How about your arms? Ribs?"

"My shoulder hurts." It throbbed, actually, as if the blood would pulse right out through her aching muscles.

"Hmm, doesn't look dislocated." Monica gave a few experimental touches.

"Ow!" Pain lanced through Rachel's shoulder.

"Hold still," Monica said grimly.

"Did you call the police for me?" Rachel asked Aunt Becca through gritted teeth.

"I spoke to Horatio personally. He's on his way."

"What happened?" Naomi demanded.

Rachel relayed what she could remember, trying to block out the memory of her terrifying flight and painful tumble.

Monica shook her head in disbelief. "Not to be mean, but you're not hurt very much considering you were rammed by a car. You should be grateful it's not worse."

"Well…" She remembered the jumbling of the bike frame as her tires skidded. "I turned back to look at the car, and my bike ran off the road because I was hugging it too closely. Maybe that made the car only sideswipe me rather than hitting me full on."

"Praise Jesus!" Becca said. "He took care of you." She wrapped her in a hug against Monica's protests.

Had God been taking care of her? Did He really care so much about her that He'd do something small like making her bike skid? Was He really orchestrating her life like that? Rachel wondered.

Her mind shied away from the thought. She had never really thought of God as that *intimately* concerned about her. She had always thought of God as a distant, powerful figure who didn't bother Himself much about her, which was a view of Him that was easier for Rachel to understand and fit into her life. Did God really care about her like that? The idea seemed foreign to her. A God who cared about her might require more of her than she'd been used to giving Him—more than going to church with her family, reading her Bible once in a while, praying once in a while. And she wasn't sure she was ready to do that.

"Did you see anything about the car?" Edward approached her again. "Make, model?"

She could barely remember that Naomi drove a Lexus and Aunt Becca drove a pink Cadillac. "No. I didn't get a good look at it."

"That's too bad."

The disappointment on his face made her spirits sink a fraction. She racked her mind, but couldn't remember more than a flash of chrome. Or was that from the first car that had passed her?

"Why are you here?" she blurted out. She wanted him here, but felt shy about telling him so, and it came out awkwardly. She'd never be as smooth with her words as Naomi or Monica.

"I went to your house this morning with a report for you about the greenhouse," Edward said. "Don't worry, I also spoke to your father about it. To reassure him."

Had he thought she couldn't relay the information herself accurately? Or had he wanted to spare her and instead put himself in the line of fire—her father's detailed grilling? Edward's closed expression couldn't tell her anything.

She opened her mouth, but the words didn't form. *I'm glad you're here but you didn't have to tag along* sounded ungracious, and her mixed emotions seemed perversely paradoxical today.

He was obviously reading her mind, because he said, "Don't worry, Rachel, I'm glad I was there when you called and could see for myself that you're okay."

His words made a smile rise to her face. "Thanks."

"There's Horatio," Aunt Becca said. She and Rachel's two sisters walked toward a car in the distance, waving their arms.

Edward glanced at their backs and leaned closer to Rachel. "I do want to ask a favor, however."

"What?"

"I want you to come with me to talk privately with your father."

Privately? "About what?" she asked, bewildered.

He glanced at her mangled bike. "About protection. For you."

"For me?"

"You're not safe. Someone may be out to kill you."

Edward followed Rachel into her father's study. Augustus Grant looked up quickly from his desk, and his body seemed to relax at the sight of her striding into the room with only a barely noticeable limp.

He navigated his wheelchair from behind the desk toward them.

"You don't have to move, Dad—"

Augustus grasped her arm and pulled her down to embrace her tightly. It seemed to surprise her, from the start she gave and the pink in her cheeks. "I'm fine, Dad."

"Well, what did you expect me to think when you call home talking about 'riding your bike' and 'car' and 'accident'?"

The man had a point. If Edward had received that kind of phone call, he'd have expected Rachel to come home looking more battered than she did.

"Edward." Augustus extended his hand to him. "Thank you for going out there for me."

Augustus's grip was still weak, but much firmer than it had been a few months ago. He seemed to be progressing steadily since the stroke.

"It was no trouble."

Rachel rolled her father to the fireplace, and she and Edward settled into chairs. Augustus settled back and rested his hands at his stomach, his gray-blond hair catching the light from the open windows.

"Augustus, I wanted to run an idea by you to get your opinion." And his permission, although Edward would find a way to go through with his plans even if Augustus protested.

"Dad, for the record, I don't think Edward's idea is necessary," Rachel said.

The older man cocked his head in question.

"There are two things about the greenhouse break-in that bother me," Edward said. "First, the man—or men, because I think there were at least two of them responsible, were professional enough to dismantle a very sophisticated security system. Second, they not only trashed the plants, I think they stole a handful of them. We're a few short."

Augustus frowned thoughtfully.

"And there's no way the thief knew the computer belonged to Naomi and not Rachel. Rachel had been carrying it and it had been stolen from *her*."

A deeper frown.

"Then the accident today—"

"You can't assume it was deliberate," Rachel interrupted. "This is Sonoma, with a winery on every corner. It's entirely possible it was a car full of tourists who were imbibing a little too much."

"This early in the morning? Most wineries don't open until 10:00 a.m."

Rachel opened her mouth, then closed it again. With her usual candor, she relented, "You're right. I don't think it was drunk tourists, either. But I also don't think I need the kind of protection you're suggesting."

"Protection?" Augustus asked.

"All these things happening makes me think someone is after Rachel's research...and maybe her life," Edward said.

Augustus nodded. "Although I'm not sure why they tried to hurt her. All they have is a basil plant, not the scar-reduction cream itself or the formulation for it."

A shadow crossed Rachel's face, and Edward

thought he could read her mind—*Except that they might have the formulation, in which case they don't need me.*

"If they were only trying to injure me, not kill me, it would set back development enough for a rival company to release their own scar-reduction cream," Rachel said.

"Regardless of whether they were trying to kill you or injure you, you need protection so they can't do it again," Edward said. He turned to Augustus. "I want to stick close to her for the next few days."

"I think it's unnecessary," Rachel said. "I'm perfectly safe inside the spa. There are card-key locks on the doors, security cameras surrounding the perimeter of the building so no one can approach without being filmed and two security guards on duty at all times."

"Which was why you were mugged right outside the back door?" Edward pointed out.

"I think the guards will be more aware and that won't happen again." But Rachel's cheeks flushed and she looked away from him.

He wondered if the real reason she was putting up resistance was because she didn't want to spend time with him. They'd been cool and polite to each other, but closer quarters might be too awkward. Nevertheless he had to do something to protect her, no matter if she didn't want him to.

"What about driving to and from the spa?" Edward asked. "Half the time you drive separately from

Naomi and your aunt Becca because you need to stay late to work." He couldn't help himself—his voice had an edge to it when he mentioned her work.

Augustus cleared his throat. "Rachel, would you leave the two of us alone?"

She looked stung as she stared at her father, but silently obeyed, closing the library door with a crisp snap.

The man pinned Edward with steely blue eyes. "You seem rather concerned for a man who only works with my daughter."

So Rachel hadn't told her family about how they'd been slowly growing closer—at least until he'd deliberately withdrawn from her. He didn't blame her, but he also wasn't going to apologize. He had never crossed the line between them.

Until today. He'd embraced her today because he hadn't been able to help himself. "When Rachel and I were in high school, we didn't hang out together, but we knew each other. And then a year ago, she hired me to grow her basil plants, and we've gotten closer as friends." He couldn't control the tic at his cheek as he spoke the word. "I simply can't stand by and do nothing when I know a friend's life could be in danger. Would you?"

Augustus eyed him steadily, then sighed. "I have to admit that having you drive Rachel, Naomi and Becca to and from the spa would ease my mind. You won't need to stay with them all day because the spa has security, but if you could be with Rachel outside the building, I would be in your debt."

"I'd also like to ride out with her every morning so she's never alone again while biking."

Augustus's eyebrows rose. "She's not going to like that."

"True, but she's a scientist. She'll eventually see the logic behind it."

But Edward wondered if it was really logic that made him want to spend this extra time with Rachel. Why did the prospect of starting his day with a bike ride with her suddenly make his days seem brighter?

THREE

"I think that car is following us."

Rachel didn't know if it was her paranoia, but it did seem that the blue car was tailing them. Every turn on the winding Sonoma roads would hide the car briefly, but then it would appear around the next bend.

Granted, these roads saw lots of traffic because there were dozens of wineries along it, almost all of them open for wine tasting to tourists. The Joy Luck Life spa itself sat in the middle of rolling hills covered with grapevines, neighbored by wineries with sometimes hundreds of visitors a day, especially in summer.

But somehow this car seemed almost sinister. Or maybe she was just being fanciful—her sisters always told her that she was too imaginative.

Edward, who was driving her to work, kept glancing in the rearview mirror for another mile. Then he said, "I think you're right."

Her stomach lurched as if they'd hit a pothole. Except they hadn't. "What? Are you sure?" She hadn't really wanted to be right.

"I think so."

She twisted around to glance through the back window. "The blue one?"

"Yes."

"I can't make out who's driving it. Too much shadow on the road from the trees."

"We're coming up to a bright patch," Edward said.

She peered intently at the windshield of the blue car, but the sunlight glinted off the glass. "Too much glare, but I think it's a man." What was happening? First the laptop was stolen, then she was run off the road, now someone was following her.

She spared a fleeting thought that she was glad she'd overslept this morning—if she had gotten up on time, Edward would also be driving Naomi and Aunt Becca to work with her. As it was, they were both already at the spa, having driven there earlier this morning because Naomi had paperwork to do.

They were safe.

But she and Edward weren't. Initially, she'd been peeved at her father's insistence that Edward be her temporary bodyguard, but then logic reasserted itself and she was glad for his protection.

Except now she realized that if someone was really after her, it put him in the line of fire. And she didn't want that.

"Let me see if I can lose him," Edward said. "Hang on."

Edward's truck suddenly veered, throwing her

against the window because she had loosened the seat belt and twisted around in her seat. Dust clouded around them for a moment before they continued down the new lane, a dirt track that was smaller than the main road they'd been on.

The car didn't follow them.

"It kept going." Rachel's heart settled back down into her chest. "I feel silly, I shouldn't have said anything in the first place."

"I don't blame you, after everything that's happened."

His approbation warmed her chilled heart.

Edward knew the Sonoma roads well enough to circle back around to the highway without needing to do a three-point turn. They were just entering the spa driveway when Rachel gasped. "There it is."

Directly in front, heading toward them from the opposite direction. As if it had driven past the spa and then turned around.

As if it had been waiting for them to arrive.

"Let's get you inside the spa quick," Edward said. He jammed the accelerator and hustled down the spa's long driveway to curve around to the staff parking lot behind the building.

"It stopped." She pointed out the back window at where the car had angled into the entrance to the driveway, but then paused. "It's not within range of the outside surveillance cameras."

"Naomi never ordered that the angle be increased?"

Edward asked. "After the two murders that happened at the spa last year?"

Rachel glared at him. "We didn't exactly expect any more situations where we'd need to videotape a car *before* it entered the spa driveway."

He parked the truck, but they still had a view of the driveway around the trees guarding the opening and the bushes lining the staff parking lot. However, neither of them moved from their seats.

She squinted at her limited view of the car, which included only a piece of the passenger side. Then she saw the door swing open. "They're getting out." Her heart rate sped up.

"Inside the spa," Edward barked.

"No, wait. They're not getting out. They just dumped something on the ground. Now they're leaving." The piece of the car that Rachel could see backed out of view, then she saw a flash of blue as the car sped down the highway.

She exhaled long and slowly, while her heartbeat thrummed against the base of her throat. Now she understood why excitement could make someone have a heart attack—hers was in overdrive. She inhaled deeply, willing herself to relax.

"What did they drop?" Edward got out of the truck and headed for the driveway.

"Wait, is that safe?" Rachel said, also getting out.

Edward returned holding aloft a laptop case. "Let's get inside." He hustled her indoors.

Naomi's office was open, and she and Aunt Becca were there enjoying a cup of tea. Naomi read Rachel's face and abruptly stood. "What happened?"

"We think we were followed."

Aunt Becca gasped. "Are you all right?"

"We're fine." Rachel took the case from Edward and laid it on Naomi's desk. "A car dropped this at the entrance to the spa driveway and took off."

"Is that our laptop?" Aunt Becca leaned over to peer at it. "The one that was just stolen?"

Naomi opened the case. The computer inside certainly looked like the one they'd just bought. On top was a note, handwritten in what seemed a childish hand.

My mom made me give this back. I'm sorry.

"Aw." A half smile softened the corners of Aunt Becca's mouth.

"Aunt Becca..." Rachel remonstrated.

"He *stole* the laptop to begin with," Naomi added.

"But he returned it."

"We should call Detective Carter," Naomi said.

Aunt Becca laid a hand on her arm. "Do we need to? The thief seems sorry."

"Just because he returned it doesn't mean he's sorry. Maybe the laptop was broken when it fell."

"Fire it up and see."

Naomi and Rachel peered at the start-up screen,

but the two accounts Naomi had created—hers and Rachel's—appeared without problems. Naomi logged in and opened the few files she had on the hard drive, which wasn't much. "It seems okay."

"See? No need to call the police."

"No, you should call them anyway," Edward chimed in. "You never know."

Naomi flipped open her cell phone. "I almost have Detective Carter on speed dial," she muttered.

Aunt Becca heaved a long-suffering sigh. "I still think this is unnecessary. That poor boy, to think he had to steal. At least he listened to his mother."

"Aunt Becca, we still don't know why he returned the laptop, and there's no proof his mama made him do it," Naomi said.

Rachel privately agreed, but on the other hand, she could relate to her aunt's feelings that it seemed a bit mean to report a laptop that was stolen but returned.

"Hello? Detective Carter? Yes, ahem…it's Naomi Grant…."

Rachel listened with half an ear, chewing her lip while faintly squirming inside at the Grant sisters needing to call the police yet again.

The greenhouse break-in had made her irrational. In light of the returned laptop, the blue car this morning made sense—the car was probably not following them at all, but had instead been heading to the spa to return the laptop. It had most likely overshot the spa driveway and turned around, appearing just as they pulled in.

And the bike accident yesterday probably *had* been drunk tourists, or tired ones.

As for the greenhouse, why was she surprised? The industry was cutthroat and her scar-reduction cream promised to be revolutionary. Dad was right, she should have taken greater precautions in the first place to guard the plants.

Naomi clicked her cell phone shut and gave Aunt Becca a superior look. "Detective Carter *thanked* us for telling him about the laptop."

Aunt Becca sniffed and rolled her eyes.

"But he also said it would be difficult to find out who stole it. They don't have enough manpower to investigate, and since it was returned, it's a low priority."

"Now I feel rather silly for being so nervous in the car," Rachel said. "I'm the one who first thought we were being followed—"

"It's nobody's fault," Edward interrupted. "We were just being cautious."

A knock at the door made them all turn. Gloria Reynolds, one of the spa's longtime clients, peered in. "Miss Grant? I wanted to see if I could schedule my appointment for an earlier time slot. But I arrived at the spa so early that the receptionists aren't at the front desk yet, so I thought I'd come here…"

Naomi had her professional smile in place as she hurried toward Gloria. "I apologize that the receptionists aren't there, Ms. Reynolds. I'm certain we can schedule you for an earlier appointment. A manicure, was it?" They disappeared from the doorway and could be heard heading down the hallway, toward the entrance foyer.

"I have a lot of work to do today," Rachel said and noticed Edward's eyes flickered away from her. The gesture was familiar to her, but she couldn't understand how or why.

No matter, she had to get to work. "Thanks for the ride, Edward."

He smiled at her, but seemed to be avoiding her eyes.

"Well, that was a bit of excitement to start the day," Aunt Becca said as he left.

"That's enough excitement for me," Rachel said as she headed toward her lab. "I'll stop being so paranoid from now on, or else I'll start thinking everything that happens to me is a threat to my life."

FOUR

"So you're driving Rachel to and from work?" Alex asked his brother.

"And any of her family who needs a lift at the same time," Edward replied.

"Do you really think she's in danger?"

Edward navigated the turn out of his farm's driveway onto the highway. "I'm not sure. But I also don't want to take any chances." Regardless of how he felt about her, he couldn't do nothing.

Alex had wanted to come along with Edward while he picked up Rachel from the spa because Alex wanted to check whether the truck's engine whined when it went over a certain speed.

A smile as bright as the July sun lit Rachel's face when she saw Alex in the truck. "Hey, stranger."

Alex got out to buss her cheek in greeting. "You don't come to the greenhouse often enough."

"I get there plenty—you're just always busy avoiding me," Rachel said playfully.

"Do your aunt and sister need a ride?" Alex asked as he got into the backseat.

"No, Aunt Becca drove them this morning. Naomi had to get to work early," Rachel said as she climbed into the truck. "They actually just left. I had to finish an experiment."

On the drive to her home, Rachel turned in her seat to talk to Alex, who was sitting behind them. As they bantered back and forth, the way they always did, Edward tried to concentrate on the traffic, which was almost nonexistent, and the road, which was smooth.

He and Rachel used to banter together before he'd started distancing himself from her.

And now he was jealous of his younger brother. He snorted in self-disgust and sped up. The faster he got her home, the better.

He pulled up to the front door and reached over to touch her arm before she climbed out of the truck. "I have something to talk to you about."

Her smooth skin contrasted with the callouses of his fingers. They were too different. He had good reason to keep his emotions in check.

She rubbed at her eyes. "Sure, but could I take my contacts out first? They're killing me."

"I'll walk you to the house."

"I'll stay in the truck," Alex said from the backseat.

"Don't be silly, Aunt Becca would love to stuff you with whatever our housekeeper baked today." Rachel shut the truck door and headed inside the Grants' large home with Edward and Alex following her.

While Rachel hurried up the wide staircase to the second story, Edward and Alex waited in the foyer.

Augustus Grant emerged from one of the doorways flanking the foyer, his wheelchair rolling smoothly on the marble tile. "Edward, Alex. How are you boys doing?"

Alex shook the man's hand first, then Edward reached out to do the same.

And jumped when he heard the scream.

The house alarm blared a half second after the scream and persisted thereafter.

Edward took the stairs three at a time. He'd never been upstairs to Rachel's room, so he hoped it was easy to find in this huge house.

It was. She stood in the hallway outside her room, frozen. She turned when she saw him, and seemed to snap out of her shock. She pointed into her room. "A man! He's escaping out my window!"

Edward glanced inside in time to see a man's booted foot disappear below her bedroom's window ledge. The intruder was diving off the sloping roof from the second story to the ground.

"What's going on?" Alex shouted over the alarm.

"An intruder." Edward ran back through the hallway, leaped down the stairs in three bounds and pelted out the front door, aware of Alex close behind him.

They rounded the front corner of the house, but Edward lost precious seconds fumbling for the latch in the wooden gate that led to the backyard.

"Never mind that," Alex said, tugging at him. "He

won't stay in the garden—he'll be headed for the woods out back."

Cursing himself for not thinking, Edward followed Alex along the wooden fence that hemmed in the Grants' extensive rose garden, toward the grove of apple trees that stood on the back end of the property. Sure enough, the man had run through the rose garden and leaped over the fence and was now hurrying toward the grove. He was only a blur—medium height, not large, but quick.

"Hurry!" Edward shouted to his taller brother, who had a longer stride. "There's a road on the other side of the grove!" Little used and perfect for parking a getaway car.

Alex obeyed and picked up speed, inching away from Edward, although he tried to keep up. They lost time weaving in between the apple trees. Edward stepped on a fallen apple and stumbled, slamming a hand against a tree to right himself, but kept going.

He emerged from the grove seconds behind Alex, just in time to see taillights heading down the road in a cloud of dead leaves and debris.

Her entire bedroom was in shambles.

Rachel had to sag against the door frame to keep herself upright. Her entire body was shaking. She felt violated.

"Oh, my goodness." Aunt Becca's voice floated to her. "Rachel, your room…"

"What happened?" roared her father from down-stairs, panic and frustration in his tone.

She felt rather than saw her sisters on either side of her. Monica grabbed her arm as if to keep her standing.

"I'll turn off the alarm," Naomi said. "Aunt Becca, call the police."

Rachel rolled around and leaned against the wall outside her bedroom. She didn't want to see it. No one said anything—they could barely hear over the ear-piercing alarm.

Where was Edward? Did he capture the intruder?

Finally, the alarm shut off. The silence was almost louder.

"How did someone get in the house?" Monica demanded.

"The window's open," said Aunt Becca.

The man had pivoted and thrown it open just as Rachel entered her bedroom. She hadn't seen his face. In her first shocked glimpse of her room, she'd only seen the mess—clothes scattered, mattress upturned and slashed, drawers in splinters, book pages littering the room. She shuddered.

"Rachel!" Edward called.

She reached for Edward automatically, wrapping her arms around him and burying her face in his shoulder. He was warm from running, musky with the scent of pine and a thread of orchid. The smell wrapped around her, a shelter in the midst of the chaos she'd seen.

His embrace was tight, protective. She just wanted him to keep holding her. She wanted him to take the ugliness away and make everything okay again.

Except that nothing would ever be okay again.

"Dad! How did you…?" Monica's shocked voice made Rachel look up.

Her father wheeled toward them, with Alex, Naomi and the housekeeper following. He hadn't been upstairs since his stroke. "Alex carried me up the stairs, and Evita and Naomi carried my wheelchair," he said. Then he saw Rachel's room and paled.

It was the only thing that could have made Rachel move away from Edward. Her father wasn't going to have a relapse, was he?

"You shouldn't be here," Monica said fiercely, reaching her father at the same time as Rachel and Naomi.

He took a few deep breaths. "I'm fine. Just surprised." He looked at Rachel then, and she thought he might have said something more to her, or maybe might have even embraced her, but then he cleared his throat and the moment was gone.

She straightened and turned away. She shouldn't have hoped for his comfort. Her father had never been very affectionate.

Evita gasped as she looked in the room. "How could this have happened?"

"We chased a man." Edward explained what had happened when he took off after the intruder who exited her room. "No one heard him ransacking her room?"

The housekeeper wrung her hands. "I was in the kitchen all afternoon. It's too far away—I wouldn't have heard anyone in her room."

"I was with Evita," Monica added. "I didn't hear anything, either."

"Me, too." Dad pounded a fist against his wheelchair. "I was in my bedroom for a few hours, then my study. The bedroom's on the opposite side of the house, and the study's on the first floor near the kitchen."

"If you keep the house alarm on, how did he get in?" Edward asked.

Naomi's brow furrowed. "Yeah, someone coming in the window would have tripped it the same way he tripped it going out."

"Wait, there was that UPS man," Monica said. "He dropped off something for Naomi."

The housekeeper nodded. "I turned off the alarm when I answered the door, but I turned it on again after he left."

"That's probably when the intruder came in." Monica said.

Despite the alarm on the house, someone had violated Rachel's private bedroom. Despite the security at the spa, someone might have infiltrated her lab and computer and stolen her research formula. And despite the alarm at the greenhouse, someone had tried to destroy her plants, crippling her product launch. She still didn't know how many of the basil plants would survive.

Her cousin Jane had said she'd finagled her boss to give her some time off from work, and she would come by tomorrow to look at Rachel's spa computer, but even with that precaution Rachel was taking, it seemed like too little, too late. Security and alarms hadn't stopped whoever was after her and her research.

She couldn't stop them.

"Where's that UPS package?" her father demanded.

"In the kitchen," Evita said. "I'll make some Japanese tea…" She eyed Edward and Alex. "And maybe some coffee, too?"

Edward seemed to hold back for a moment as they all trooped downstairs. Rachel glanced up at him, suddenly self-conscious about the way she'd hurled herself into him. "Edward?" Maybe he felt it, too, this awkward aftermath. No, he snatched at her hand.

"Are you all right?" Edward asked.

She shrugged, not wanting him to worry about her. But she also knew him well enough to know that if she didn't tell the truth, he'd worry even more. "I'm still a bit shaken, I think. It's hard." She swallowed and glanced at the open doorway to her room, unwilling to look inside again.

He squeezed her hand, then let go. "A mug of tea will warm you up." He ushered her downstairs.

When they entered the kitchen, at first Rachel thought something was wrong because everyone huddled around the breakfast table. She peered over Naomi's shoulder and saw Alex tinkering with a gilded porcelain confection. "What is that?"

"A music box," said Aunt Becca. "It came in the UPS package for Naomi."

"Was there a note?" Edward asked.

Naomi nodded. "Just a short typewritten one. 'From an admirer.'"

Rachel eyed the box with incredulity. "Did they hope we wouldn't connect the package with the break-in?"

"It might be unrelated," her father said slowly. "Whoever broke into your room could have simply been waiting for anyone to turn off the alarm so he could sneak in."

"A bit risky," Edward speculated. "If no one had showed up all day, the only time the alarm went off would be when Rachel got home."

Dad shook his head slowly. "I usually go out into the garden in the early afternoon. I didn't today because I had too much work to do."

Rachel shuddered. Monica voiced her thoughts. "If you had, the man would have entered sooner, with just you, me and Evita at home."

"Then praise God," Aunt Becca said. "At least this way, he tripped the alarm when Edward and Alex were here and could at least catch a glimpse of him."

"It wasn't much of a glimpse," Edward muttered.

"I think I found something," Alex said.

They leaned in to see. He held out his hand, in which rested some small electronic device that reminded Rachel of a crumpled metallic spider. "What is that?"

Alex shook his head. "Not sure, but it doesn't belong in the music box." He gestured to the mess on the table—the porcelain housing, an assortment of gears and screws and other things Rachel didn't understand.

"Are you sure?" Aunt Becca asked.

"Alex is a whiz at electronic and mechanical things," Edward said.

Rachel nodded. At the greenhouse, she'd seen him repair both delicate electronics and tinker with his car engine. "I trust his judgment."

The doorbell rang. Everyone froze for a moment, then Aunt Becca laughed at herself. "That's probably Horatio. He mentioned he was nearby when I talked to him."

Rachel gave her statement to Detective Carter, whose gentle gray eyes seemed to understand how terrible she felt about everything that had happened. At one point, he even touched her arm briefly. "I hate to ask this, but have you looked through your room to see if anything is missing?"

"I haven't even gone inside yet," she whispered.

He gave a small smile. "After my officers have collected any evidence, try to steel yourself and start cleaning up. And let me know if you notice anything unusual." He squeezed her forearm. "Buck up, Rachel. It'll be okay."

His kindness buoyed her.

"I'll check on the UPS truck, too," he promised her.

"Thank you, Detective."

As he was leaving, he saw Edward hovering nearby. "Edward, I forgot to call you to ask—did you get around to figuring out if any plants were taken from your greenhouse?"

"Actually…" Edward's face vacillated between pale and red. He placed his hands on Rachel's shoulders as if to brace her. "I, uh, was going to talk to you about that before…"

Yes, he had wanted to speak to her when they first drove up to the house. She tried to answer, but her throat had dried. She swallowed painfully. "Well?" she croaked.

His eyes were pained—for her. "There are three plants missing."

"Three? Are you sure?" Detective Carter asked.

"Alex and I cleaned out greenhouse four, and counted all the plants several times. We checked the grounds around the greenhouses, in case the plants were dropped by the intruders or by one of us." His thumbs rubbed her skin once, twice. "There are three plants gone."

As the shock wore off, Rachel became aware of a rising sense of hope. "They stole three plants. They *needed* to steal three plants." Her breath started to come quickly. "That means they didn't know what strain of basil it was. That means…"

Edward caught on. "We thought they only intended to sabotage your product launch. They shouldn't have needed to take samples."

"If they already had my research notes, they'd already have known the basil strain. Edward, that means they don't know. That means they might not have stolen my research yet." Rachel's hands flew up to grip his forearms. "We still have a chance to save this product launch."

FIVE

She had a chance, and she wasn't going to waste it.

Rachel approached her research associate, Stephanie, where she was doing quality-control tests on the last batch of scar-reduction cream at her lab bench. "Stephanie, I need to use your computer."

Stephanie paused in her pipetting and peered up at her through her owl-like glasses. "Jane is still working on yours?"

Rachel nodded and held up a flash drive. "And I have new clinical trial data to sort through that can't wait." Especially not now that time seemed to be slipping away like sand in an hourglass. She needed to finish the final verification on the formulation's efficacy and ready it for mass production soon.

Stephanie gestured toward her computer at her desk. "Go ahead. Although I'll have this quality-control data ready to download in a couple hours."

"I'll be done by then." Rachel sat at Stephanie's desk, amazed as always by the Spartan neatness. She could barely see the surface of her own desk for all the papers littering it.

After she'd been working for a little while, she heard the centrifuge fire up. Then a shadow fell across the screen and Stephanie leaned against the desk edge, obviously waiting for the separator to finish its run. "So, how's the formulation coming along?"

For some reason, the innocent question jangled through her. *Don't be silly.* Rachel had worked with Stephanie for two years, now, for goodness' sake. Everything was making her paranoid. "I'm almost done. It's hard to scale it up for larger production."

"I figured." Stephanie smiled. "This will be the first product launch that I have worked with you. The last formula didn't make it this far."

The ill-fated diamond-dust cleanser. Rachel couldn't help the cloud over her soul at the remembrance of her father's bitter words after that failure. "This is ten times better than that cleanser."

"Seems that way. You spent an awful lot of time on the formulation for this."

Again, that frisson of distrust that ran through her. Rachel glanced up at her assistant, but Stephanie had the same placid smile. Was it just her imagination that there was a faint edge to that smile, some tension around her eyes? Rachel's hand gripped the computer mouse, her nails scraping the plastic. "The time I put in will be worth it," she said mildly.

"Did you need any help?" Stephanie asked.

Something inside Rachel stilled for a long moment, her heart seemed to pound harder and faster than before.

Stephanie was a good research assistant, but never proactive or inquisitive about the formulation process. Her background was Quality Control and Quality Assurance, not chemistry or formulation, and certainly not dermatology.

And she had never asked to help before.

Rachel faltered. She should just be polite, tell her no and forget about it. But she didn't want to forget about it. She wanted to ask Stephanie why she was suddenly so interested. The question bubbled up in her gut until it was almost at her lips. Then her office door opened.

"Rachel? I finished." Jane's smiling face peered around the door.

Rachel took the time to remove the clinical data from Stephanie's computer even though it didn't have anything critical, but her suspicions were buzzing too loud in her ears for her to ignore.

She closed the office door behind her and sat next to Jane in front of her computer. "So, what did you find?"

Jane bit her lip and glanced at Rachel. "I hate to tell you this, but your computer was hacked into two years ago."

At first, the word *hacked* seemed to cut into her chest, but then she registered *two years ago* and breathed easier. "Not recently?"

Jane shook her head, her straight chin-length hair swinging against her jaw, drawing Rachel's attention to the scars there. Or maybe Rachel was just sensitive to them.

After all, she had caused them.

But this scar-reduction cream would make up for that fire in the playhouse.

"I couldn't find out who had gained access to the computer," Jane was said, "and I couldn't figure out which files."

"I would just assume the hacker stole all my research notes." Why else break into her office and her computer? She glanced at the door, guarded only by a doorknob lock. Stupid! Why hadn't she gotten a dead bolt, or even better, installed a heavy card-key door like the ones guarding the lab area at the back of the spa from the front clientele areas?

"Whoever did it, however, didn't erase the time stamp. A little over two years ago, September 19, 9:07 p.m."

Rachel wrote it down, but as she did, each letter and number seemed to burn into the page.

Her greenhouse. Her bedroom. Her office.

Her life.

"This isn't happening." She was surprised at how tight her voice was, then realized her teeth were clenched.

Jane's eyes and mouth softened. "Do you want to talk about it?"

"I've been talking about it, and it hasn't helped. Because no one can do anything about it."

"God can do something about it." Jane touched her hand. "You're not all alone in facing this."

Rachel shifted her hand away. "I feel alone in this. My life has been violated and there's nothing I can do to change how that makes me feel."

"There is something you can do. You can pray."

"How would that help anything?" Rachel retorted fiercely. "Why would God even care?"

Jane swallowed. "He does care, Rachel."

"Well, it certainly doesn't seem that way." She firmed her mouth. "If He cared, He wouldn't have allowed all these horrible things to happen to me."

"You know that's not fair."

"I'm tired of being a scientist, of being logical and practical and fair. Jane, they stole my research!" Her hand whipped out and smacked the computer monitor.

"Hey, hey." Jane grabbed her hand and held it.

The warmth of her fingers calmed Rachel down some. "I'm sorry, I didn't mean to throw a tantrum."

Jane smiled. "You're usually so calm, Rach. But this cream has you more upset than I've ever seen you. It must be important."

Rachel's eyes flickered to Jane's scars again, and this time her cousin noticed. Jane's eyes darkened and she seemed to stifle a sigh. "Rachel, why are you still hung up over that fire?"

"Jane, it was a *fire*."

"But I'm fine."

"You're not."

Jane blinked at Rachel's harsh tone. "Rach, I'm fine about the scars. Really. I could have had plastic surgery years ago to remove them, but I didn't want to because I don't care. You shouldn't care, either."

Jane was just being nice about it all. Rachel couldn't help but see those scars every time she saw her cousin. This scar-reduction cream would make up for the fact that she had inadvertently started that playhouse fire.

It would make up for a lot of things. "This cream is important to Dad and the spa."

"What does this data have to do with the cream now? Remember, it was two whole years ago. What did they steal?"

Rachel stilled, blinking at the monitor. Jane was right. Two years ago, she hadn't even started working full-time on the scar-reduction cream. She'd been toying with several different options. "The diamond-dust cleanser. About that time was the tail end of those experiments. They didn't go well at all—too abrasive no matter what medium I suspended them in."

"See? The stolen data probably has nothing to do with the greenhouse break-in and everything else."

"But if the research notes they had were two years old, why steal my basil plants to begin formulation now, when I'm about to launch my scar cream in a few months? They would just be trying to play catch-up—it would take a rival lab eighteen months at least to develop their own formulation and test it."

Jane shrugged. "Maybe they thought it was worth it?"

Rachel considered, then discarded the idea. "No, it wouldn't give them a good enough return on the cost for development." She stared hard at the monitor, although it told her nothing. "I need to find out exactly what they stole. Maybe I'm wrong and I already had preliminary formula notes for the scar-reduction cream. Still…" She frowned.

Jane finished her thought. "If they had a preliminary formula, it doesn't answer why they needed the basil plants."

What was it about that basil? Rachel had a murky feeling in her gut that she needed to find the answer.

And fast.

The problem with being high in demand was that occasionally he had demanding clients.

Edward tried to pay attention to the road. He probably shouldn't be driving while talking to his high-maintenance client, but Jason Witherspoon had called him on his cell phone just as he left to pick up Rachel from the spa. "Jason, you are always welcome to fly into Sonoma, but I can assure you, the orchids are doing very well."

"Well, that article I just read seemed to imply they need a higher humidity level," the multimillionaire whined.

Edward had to bite his tongue, preventing him from snapping that the writer had made some other gross errors in the article, so he wasn't likely to believe the suggestion about proper humidity levels. "I've tried different levels, but this species grows successfully at the humidity levels they're at now."

"But have you tried what this article is suggesting?" Jason persisted.

Edward sighed as he pulled into the spa parking lot. "Jason, you have only twenty plants of this orchid species. Did you really want me to risk one of them by trying to grow them according to the article? There's a chance it'll die."

The prospect of losing an expensive plant sobered his client. "Well...I've already landed at the airstrip. I'll be at the farm in about half an hour."

"I might be a little late." Edward cut the engine and got out of the truck. "Alex will show you around."

"I'd rather you did, in case I had questions."

Or complaints. Edward shoved aside the unkind thought. Jason hadn't become a successful CEO without questioning and pushing for improvements in whatever he worked on. "I'm sorry, but when you called, I was already out on an errand. I'll be there in about forty-five minutes."

"I suppose I'll just wait," he said peevishly.

"Tell you what, I'll ask Alex to warm up some

of Mama's apricot *empanadas*. She made some last night."

Jason loved Edward's mother and viewed her as a Hispanic version of Emeril. He especially loved her mini fruit turnovers, so this put him in a good mood. *"Empanadas?"* he asked, his voice sounding twenty years younger. "All right, don't hurry on my account." He hung up.

Despite his client's words, Edward knew he needed to get Rachel home pronto or even Mama's *empanadas* wouldn't be sweet enough for Jason's mood. He entered the spa through the staff entrance and then the card key area.

"Rachel?" he called as he entered the lab. "I hate to rush you, but…"

She sat in her office in front of the computer, seemingly in thought, but something about her posture—maybe the hunched set of her shoulders, the weak tilt of her head—told Edward she wasn't all right. His impatience drained away, and he reached out to touch her shoulder, trying to tell her that he was there for her.

"Rachel?"

Her shoulder seemed to relax under his touch, but her entire body still heaved in a shuddering breath. Up close, he could see that her hands were faintly shaking. He spun her chair around so he could see her face.

She wasn't crying, but her pale cheeks and trembling lips told him that she was teetering on the verge of tears. He couldn't help himself, and he cupped her face in his hand, his fingers tangling in her hair. "Tell me."

She shook her head, her soft skin rubbing his palm. "I'm just being silly."

"There's nothing silly in everything that's happened to you."

"It's worse," she whispered.

The words made him want to stand over her and fight off her enemies. "What happened?"

She gestured toward the computer. "Jane said someone hacked into my computer about two years ago."

"So they didn't get any recent data? That's a good thing, right?"

She gave him a half smile. "Yes, I suppose so. But it doesn't explain why they stole my basil plants, why they wanted to ruin the launch."

"They might have trashed the greenhouse because they're jealous of your success." The word made something harden inside him, but he knew her success meant a great deal to her, even if he didn't agree with her priorities in order to get it.

Rachel, however, gave a short cynical bark. "Is that what you think?"

"What do you mean?"

A tear cascaded down her cheek. Then another. "I'm a failure."

He brushed the tears away. He'd never heard her speak in such a despairing tone. "What are you talking about? You're not. You really believe that?" He immediately regretted his raw words, afraid they'd only hurt her more.

But Rachel just shook her head. "I've done nothing but fail my father."

"That can't be true." What had Naomi and Becca told him? "The spa is known for the skin-care products you created."

She bit her lip and shut her eyes, another tear falling onto his fingers.

While she was unaware of his gaze, he stared at her face, delicate, vulnerable, beautiful. He wanted to lean in and press a kiss to her soft cheek, to her lips, to erase the sadness from her mouth.

He paused.

Then he dropped his hands from her face but twined her limp fingers in his.

She opened her eyes, turning her head to gaze unseeing at the computer. "Two years ago, the data that was stolen was for a diamond-dust cleanser that failed miserably. And before that was the Avignon scandal."

"What?" The name Avignon sounded familiar, but he couldn't remember where he'd heard it.

She turned to face him with wide, anguished eyes. "Everyone was gossiping about it." She explained about the two grape-seed extract moisturizers that Joy Luck Life and Avignon spa had developed separately, and how Joy Luck Life had been accused of "stealing" Avignon's formula.

Now he remembered. People had been whispering

about the scandal. Most Sonoma residents were out-raged at the impugning of their most popular local spa, but a few people and many tourists thought Joy Luck Life had done something underhanded. "That was just bad luck. It doesn't mean you're a failure."

"Dad wasn't happy."

The sentence itself wasn't unusual or unexpected. Edward knew Augustus Grant was a good business-man who would demand as much from his daughters as any other employee. But the way she said it implied something deeper, as if her heart were breaking.

"Dad blamed me for going through with the prod-uct launch the month after Avignon released their moisturizer. He said the negative press cast aspersions on the spa's integrity and quality of products." She paused, swallowing hard. "We lost several wealthy clients because of it."

"But that wasn't your fault." Anger started to simmer in him. Did Augustus blame his daughter for a bad coincidence?

"He's just…" She stifled a sob. "He's so hard to please. No matter how hard I work, I never seem to please him."

Edward reached out to embrace her, and she clung tightly to him, not crying, but not okay.

No matter how hard I work…

For Edward, her words were like the first sliver of light cutting through the dark of early morning. Was this, then, the reason why she worked so hard? He'd thought her workaholic tendencies were just like his father—a selfish desire for more success, more personal satisfaction—but maybe her reasons for working so hard were different. Maybe she was only trying to live up to Augustus's expectations, or her perception of them. Edward couldn't quite reconcile the jovial image he had of her father with the exacting one she spoke of.

Then again, he had noticed several days ago the tension between father and daughter.

"I don't know how to tell him about this," she mumbled into his shirt. "He'll be so upset."

He ached for her. How to tell her that even if she never lived up to other people's expectations—her father's expectations—that God the Father will always love her?

"And it's even worse than this." She pulled away, her expression so hopeless that he wanted to kiss it away.

"How?"

"I know who stole my data." She tapped at her keyboard and a face popped up on the monitor. "Steve Schmidt. He was a research assistant I hired two years ago. He came with a great résumé, and he was competent but strangely lazy. He only worked here a week."

"A week? Did he leave?"

"No, I fired him. He snuck his girlfriend into the lab one night. We only had one security guard on duty back then, and Martin caught them when he was making his hourly rounds. I fired Steve the next day, but according to the time stamp Jane found on my computer, my research was stolen that night. By Steve."

"Or his 'girlfriend.' Rachel, that isn't your fault."

"But it is." She gripped his hands. "Don't you see? Dad has always prided himself on being a good judge of character and hiring loyal staff workers. But I…" She glanced at Steve's picture again. "I messed up when I hired Steve. I jeopardized my own research."

"You yourself said he was competent."

"But Dad will say I should have suspected something was wrong when I interviewed him." She rubbed her forehead. "Dad always had great instincts when he interviewed prospective employees."

"He didn't interview Steve?"

"No, I insisted on doing it myself. I wanted to prove to him that I could."

Edward could clearly see she had wanted to please her father.

Her mouth trembled. "He was already upset when I fired Steve after only a week. But this… Oh, Edward, I'm so afraid to tell him," she whispered.

Their eyes met then, and he stopped breathing. The expression in her hazel eyes, normally so confident and filled with intelligence, touched him like a featherlight caress to his jaw. The urge to reach out to her and kiss away all her problems rose up in him again, stronger than it had been before. He wanted to hold her, shield her. He wanted her to be his.

But no, she wasn't his. He shouldn't be thinking about that.

He dropped his gaze to their clasped hands and rubbed his thumb against her knuckles. "Let me come with you when you talk to your father."

She paused, then slowly straightened in her chair, looked him in the eye with resolution. "No. I have to do it myself." Her voice shook slightly, but she swallowed hard. "Let's go."

They were silent on the drive home. Edward ignored two calls from Jason to his cell phone.

This brief glimpse into her feelings about her father had been painful for her but enlightening to him. It had shown him a reason for her work priorities that had never occurred to him before.

It had shown him that she might be different from his father, who had missed every major event in Edward's life because Papa had been more interested in his work, in making money, in gaining promotions and working on new projects at his job. Papa had missed Edward's high school and college graduations. He had missed three out of every four of Edward's birthdays. And he had missed the one thing Edward had been most proud of, the grand opening of his greenhouse business, without even a call to explain why he hadn't shown up.

But Edward was starting to wonder if maybe Rachel's focus on her work wasn't motivated by the same things as his father's focus on his work.

Had Edward misjudged her?

SIX

"I tried Steve Schmidt's old contact information, but he's moved. So I asked Jane to try to find him," Rachel told Naomi near the end of the following workday as the two of them headed toward her sister's office. Rachel glanced at her watch—Edward was coming to pick her up soon, so she needed to collect her things from her office. The locked doors to her lab were at the end of the corridor where Naomi's office was, so they had met as Naomi had finished her last massage client.

"Do you think she can?" They turned the corner and Naomi dug her office keys out of her pocket.

They both stopped.

A spa patron stood a few yards down the hallway from Naomi's office door, in front of the double doors guarding the lab area. That in itself was unusual—spa patrons occasionally got lost in the hallways while trying to find the lounge areas, but this corridor, unlike the other spa corridors, was stark and brightly lit, unadorned by the silks, hall tables and flowers that lined the other public areas of the spa. It made it very obvious this was not the way to a lounge room or a treatment room.

What was more, this man hunched over the card-key pad on the wall to the right of the doors, his fingers scrabbling with the lock.

Trying to get into her lab.

Rachel wanted to demand what he was doing, but Naomi must have known her thoughts because she laid a hand on her arm and instead addressed the man. "Sir, can we help you?"

He flinched and straightened up, his blue eyes fastening on them for a long heartbeat.

Then he bolted.

He shot between the two of them, shoving Rachel hard against the wall. Naomi, stronger than her sister because of years of massage-therapy work, wasn't so easily tossed aside and tried to grab him, but he slithered away.

"Stop!"

Naomi and Rachel took off after him.

However, he didn't know the spa well, because he turned down the wrong hallway toward the lounge areas. He approached the door to the Tamarind lounge just as it opened. A client, Gloria Reynolds, emerged directly in the man's path.

Rachel shouted, "Stop him!" but Naomi groaned, "Oh, no."

Rachel discovered the reason for her dismay as the man realized he'd reached a dead end, with only the women's restroom doors ahead of him. He turned and wildly grabbed at Gloria, who shrieked.

"Let her go," Naomi said as they stopped a few feet away.

Rachel stared into Gloria's horrified eyes for a brief moment before the man shoved the woman into the two sisters.

Footsteps raced past them as the man escaped.

"I should have called Martin when we first saw him," Naomi said as they got to their feet.

Rachel felt a pang of guilt that she hadn't thought to do so. She never managed to think as pragmatically as her sisters, especially when it really counted. "I'll call him now." She pulled out her cell phone from her pocket and dialed the security guards' desk, although it was probably already too late.

Naomi headed down the hallway after the man.

"Hey!"

That was Edward's voice, filtering down the hallway from the spa entrance. For a moment her heart hitched and she wanted to shout to tell him to stay away in case the man hurt him. But then she realized he might be able to hinder him until the security guards got there.

"Hello? Hello?" said a voice over her cell phone.

"Martin, come quick! There's a man headed toward the entrance foyer."

Rachel couldn't hear the security guard very well because Gloria Reynolds had yet to rise from the ground and was screeching, "What was that? Who let that man in here?"

The door to the Tamarind lounge now opened. "What's going on?" asked several clients as they peered down at Gloria, still hysterical on the ground.

Rachel was surprised Naomi hadn't thought to mollify Ms. Reynolds before chasing after the man—after all, as acting manager, she usually put the clientele before everything else.

Well, then, she'd do the honors. She wasn't as tactful as Naomi, but she could at least be polite. "Are you okay, Ms. Reynolds? Are you hurt?"

"I ache all over," she snapped.

"Can you stand, or would you like to just sit there for a while?" Oh, that didn't come out right.

"I demand to know what's going on," Gloria said, thrusting out a hand so Rachel could help her to her feet.

"Well, that man—" No, she needed to be a bit more tactful, especially in front of the other Tamarind members. "We'll find out soon, Ms. Reynolds. We're very sorry for the, uh…inconvenience." My goodness, she couldn't do Naomi's job unless it didn't involve talking. She hoped she wasn't upsetting Ms. Reynolds even more.

Gloria sniffed and pushed at her highlighted locks. Luckily she didn't realize how wild they looked, although one of the other women snickered softly.

"Dr. Grant!" Several massage therapists, aestheticians and clients raced around the corner, coming from the hallways with the treatment rooms. "We heard someone scream."

"Everything's all right now," Rachel said. "Haley, could you please take care of Ms. Reynolds? I need to find out what happened." And she left them to race to the front foyer.

No sign of the strange man, but Naomi stood at the receptionists' desk, talking urgently on the phone. And Edward stood in the middle of the room, his hands held awkwardly at his sides.

"Edward! Are you all right?"

He smiled at her. "I'm fine, but don't touch me. I scratched the man and have his DNA under my nails. Naomi's calling Detective Carter right now."

That was smart of Edward, but the problem was that the Sonoma police department was very small and outsourced their DNA testing. Rachel had paid for DNA testing herself for the Malaysian basil plant and used the same lab they did, and it took over a month to get the results.

Well, maybe the police could put a rush on it.

"Rachel, what did you do with Ms. Reynolds?" Naomi's tone implied Rachel had done something wrong, and she had a sinking feeling in her stomach.

"I left her with Haley. I'm sorry, was that wrong?"

Naomi sighed. "I should have told you to stay with her and coddle her a bit, maybe stick her in one of the Saffron lounges with some wine."

Oh, that made sense, to put her in one of the elite lounges to mollify her. Rachel bit her lip. She should have thought of that herself. The spa prided itself on exemplary customer service and luxuriant pampering, and leaving a distraught client with a massage therapist hadn't been the most gracious thing to do.

"I'll take care of it."

Naomi left just as the two security guards entered through the front doors. "Sorry, he got away."

"But we got the license-plate number and make and model of the car," said Martin. "Blue Ford Taurus."

Edward had gone rigid, and he gave Rachel a long, hard look. She shivered and wrapped her arms around herself. They thought a blue car had followed them to the spa the other day.

Detective Carter arrived within a few minutes. They seemed to be calling him so often lately, he probably didn't roam beyond a ten-mile radius of the spa.

After questioning Naomi and Rachel, he dispatched an officer to process the DNA under Edward's fingernails, but he affirmed what Rachel had already suspected. The Sonoma police department outsourced their DNA testing and wouldn't have the results for a month or more.

Detective Carter then questioned everyone else, starting with the security guards, and finally spoke with Gloria Reynolds, whose pinched mouth conveyed her distaste at everything that had happened.

As Naomi and Rachel stood several yards away and

watched Gloria and Detective Carter, Naomi suddenly started. "Rach," she whispered.

"What?"

"I just remembered something from all that stuff that happened last year."

That "stuff" being two murders in the spa, Naomi being framed for them and Naomi's boyfriend Devon's life in danger. "I would think you don't like remembering all that."

"No, this is important. Do you remember that Devon and I went to talk to Gloria Reynolds because one of the murder victims had argued with her? At the end of our interview with Gloria, she mentioned something vague about dinner with our family, but she wanted to talk to *you*."

"Me? I barely know her."

"She said she wanted to talk to you about your research. Have you talked with her about it?"

Rachel searched her memory. "Most of my conversations with her are just polite chitchat."

"Rach, she specifically mentioned some diamond-dust cleanser. Does that mean anything to you?"

Rachel's stomach clenched and held, making it hard for her to take a breath for a moment. "That's right, now I remember you mentioned that to me last year. I wondered how she knew about it, but I got so distracted, I never thought much about it beyond that."

"You didn't tell her about it?"

"No. I never speak about my research. And

all my research assistants sign a confidentiality agreement."

The main focus of Rachel's stolen research notes had been about the diamond-dust cleanser. How had Gloria known about it?

Was Gloria Reynolds behind everything that had happened?

Later that day, Evita's grim face when she met Rachel at the garage door made her insides rumble darkly. "Miss Rachel, your father wanted to talk to you as soon as you got home from work."

Naomi moved in front of Rachel as if to protect her. "Why?"

"Now, Naomi, don't shoot the messenger." Aunt Becca's dark eyes reproached her.

Naomi glanced at her aunt, then gave the housekeeper a rueful half smile. "Sorry, Evita. But he already hollered the house down last night with Rachel."

"I appreciate it, but I'm not your lion cub, Naomi." Rachel sighed, although her heart fluttered.

Naomi muttered something that sounded like, "It's not fair…" but Rachel didn't quite understand what she meant by that.

"Evita, Edward's parking his truck right now, but I invited him in for some coffee," Aunt Becca said.

Evita nodded. "I thought you might. I made coffee cake, too." She gave Rachel a soft look. "Come get a piece, Miss Rachel, when you're done talking to your father."

"Where is he? His office?"

"The garden walk."

Her shoulders relaxed slightly as she headed outside. He might be in a better mood among Mom's roses.

Mom had always understood Rachel better than her father did. Rachel missed her still, even fifteen years after cancer had taken her to Jesus.

Last night had been horrible. After telling Dad what she'd learned about Steve Schmidt hacking into her computer, he had accused her of poor judgment, of failing him and the spa. Again. But he couldn't blame her more than she had already blamed herself. She'd been too dejected to want to defend herself, not that she had much to say, so she let him rant on. Their conversation had been cut short by Monica's coming in to insist Dad hadn't been doing well all day and needed to rest. Rachel knew Monica interrupted them in order to save her older sister from more of their father's anger.

The chill of the late-fall breeze stung her cheeks but carried the faint scent of the dying roses, a melancholic wave washing over her. Before Mom died, Rachel spent a lot of time out here with her, and often Dad had joined them. She and her father had been closer then.

He hadn't noticed her yet, wheeling his chair down the paved garden walk, his mouth pulled down. She swallowed. What a contrast, those carefree days and these tense ones. When had their relationship changed to this?

"Dad."

He looked up and saw her. The lines around his mouth seemed to deepen.

She steeled herself. "You wanted to talk to me?"

"Detective Carter called me to tell me about the man at the spa today."

Rachel sighed. But really, why shouldn't the detective call the spa owner to tell him about it?

"It makes me wonder why one of my own daughters or my sister-in-law Becca didn't tell me about it."

She winced. "I'm sorry, Dad."

But as silence fell between them and she waited for him to speak, she stared hard at a full-blown red rose, still bright and full. For something like that, why did he need to only speak to her? Why not Naomi, the acting manager at the spa? That seemed unreasonable. "That's not why you wanted to speak to me, Dad. What is it?"

His eyebrows rose slightly at her firm tone, making her almost apologize for her words…but not quite.

He gestured to his lap, at a file folder there. "I asked Naomi to give me Steve Schmidt's employee records."

A frisson of fire passed through her body. Suddenly she didn't want to be the same compliant daughter she always was, because this really wasn't her fault. That slim file folder—that concrete example of how little he trusted or respected her—seemed to embody all that was wrong in how he perceived her. That file folder was the last straw. "Dad, you can't blame me for this. His credentials were excellent."

"They were too good." He frowned at her, then opened the folder and frowned down at it. "You should have seen that."

"Too good?" The breeze didn't seem so cold anymore. "So you'd rather I'd have hired someone less competent?"

"You should have been suspicious."

"And you're being silly."

The words were like a bomb, because Rachel couldn't hear anything for a moment after she said them—not the wind, not the birds, not even the faint voices of Naomi, Aunt Becca and Edward coming from the open kitchen window.

Last night she'd meekly internalized his criticism. But *today*—her father seeming to blame her for the man trying to break into the lab, asking Naomi for Steve Schmidt's file as if he could do more than she had done—she'd been through too much. She'd been through too much this whole week. He'd been upset at her too much this week for her to continue to care.

Her father's eyes had widened and his jaw tensed. Normally that would have sent her frantically apologizing, but now it only fueled her temper. "You can't have it both ways, Dad. You're trying to lay all this on me, but I'm not responsible. I acted in good judgment."

"How can you know human nature when you're fussing around in that lab all day?" he roared.

Fussing? "What do you think I do all day, sit around and play with Bunsen burners?" Didn't he realize how hard she worked? How she pushed herself to shave hours off experiments so she could process the data faster? That her efforts had enabled her to develop this scar-cream formulation within months rather than years?

His mouth worked, unable to answer her. Rendering her father speechless somehow made her feel more powerful than she ever had before. "You can see Naomi taking clients, scheduling staff, organizing the spa. You can understand Monica's long work hours at the hospital. Do you really think I'm just wasting time in that lab? Don't you understand the nature of research work?"

"I understand the bottom line, and you've had two failed products—"

"I have one successful product in production and a bad coincidence with Avignon spa," she snapped. "The diamond-dust cleanser was just like any other product I've tried and discarded over the years. Research is like that."

"Well, business isn't—"

"If you wanted a businessman, you should have hired one to be the dermatologist researcher at the spa." She paused, her breath coming in shallow gasps. "Except a businessman wouldn't come up with anything creative or unique because he's a businessman. I'm a researcher."

They glared at each other. He looked at her as if he didn't recognize her, and maybe he didn't—she was the quiet one, not firm like Naomi or fiery like Monica. Well, she might be different from her sisters, but that didn't mean he could be like this to her. He might be a strong personality himself, but she wasn't going to take it anymore. She wasn't going to let him treat her this way.

She had long ago stopped wondering why he did.

He broke their tense eye contact first. He scowled at the file folder. "I should have hired the research assistant myself."

If he had said that last night, she probably would have bowed her head and taken it. But Rachel was a different woman today. "You don't know what qualities make a good research assistant, Dad."

"Now, see here—"

"No, *you* see. You might be a good judge of character, but you wouldn't know the first thing about what kind of person makes a good research assistant. And I'd be the one stuck working with him. No, Dad." She sliced her hand through the air. "I hired a competent worker, who obviously had angled to be hired specifically in order to steal my research. And unless you gave him a lie-detector test, too, even you wouldn't have known that."

"You have no call for that kind of sass, young

lady," he raged. "I'm only trying to help you do something."

"You're trying to push me as if I'm not doing anything. I'm doing everything I can, Dad."

He looked away.

Rachel turned away, too, staring at the forlorn rosebushes, most of the blooms losing their faded petals. She shivered. "I'm going inside, Dad. Don't stay out in the cold too long."

She strode away from him, shoulders back, but quaking inside. A hand brushed a rosebush, scratching her lightly, and tired pink petals rained down on the walkway.

She'd never feel solace in the garden again.

Edward hadn't meant to overhear, but Evita had left the kitchen window open to air out a faint grease smell, and he couldn't miss the raised voices.

He had never heard Rachel shout like that. Ever.

But recalling what she'd said yesterday about her father, he wondered if it had been inevitable. With all that had happened, and all she was feeling, she'd been a ticking bomb. And after she'd given him a hint as to her relationship with her father, Edward suspected that Augustus Grant would be the one most likely to set her off.

They'd all heard Rachel's parting shot. Becca looked faintly uncomfortable, but Naomi had a sparkle in her eye, although her face was neutral.

"I'm sorry, Edward," Becca said.

"I'm not," Naomi retorted.

"Naomi!" Becca was shocked.

She shrugged it off. "Edward works with her. He ought to know the kind of pressure she's been under outside work."

"I'll go talk to her." Becca slid off her chair.

"I think you ought to go talk to Dad," Naomi said. "And let Rachel cool off."

Her aunt hesitated, but then gave a slight nod and left the kitchen.

Before the silence became too awkward, Edward said, "I'll head home."

"I'm sorry that our family drama has made you uncomfortable." Naomi gave him a bright look he couldn't quite interpret. "But you did get yourself in the middle of things when you offered to drive Rachel to work."

He grunted, but softened it with a small smile as he rose from the kitchen table. "I'll see you tomorrow."

He headed out the front door to his truck, parked on the side of the Grants' long driveway, but a thought whispered at his mind as he looked at the serene landscaping in the wide front lawn.

He knew where Rachel would be.

There was a small artificial copse to one side of the property. He'd never been there himself, but Rachel had mentioned once in passing that she'd been there one morning as the sun rose. There was a good chance she went there often.

A stifled sob floated on the wind toward him just as his foot crunched a dead branch hidden in the carpet of fallen leaves. He winced, but it was probably for the best that he didn't surprise her.

She sat on a park bench artfully placed under an apple tree, and she didn't bother to hide her tear-stained face. For some reason, that made his heart warm like a rock in the sun.

He sat next to her, putting an arm around her shoulders. She sank into him, her tears running down her cheeks.

He let her cry as long as she needed to. He wasn't sure what else to do or say, but he was spurred by the warrior in him that had wanted to storm out to that garden to shield her from her father's accusing words.

Except she'd fought back, something he wouldn't have expected of her. And it had made him proud of her.

But now he held her, trying to be her strength when she needed it.

As she quieted and the wind made the tears on his shirt chill his skin, her voice drifted up to him. "He doesn't love me."

The despair, the pain of abandonment in her voice, pulled his arms tight around her. "He does love you, Rach. You can't believe that he doesn't."

"No matter how hard I try, he's never pleased with me. I can never do anything right."

Edward had to admit that Augustus seemed overly

demanding of his eldest daughter, and he didn't quite understand why. But he also remembered the concern in her father's eyes when Rachel's room had been ransacked and he came upstairs, wheeling down the hall, to see Edward holding her. Augustus's hand had lifted a few inches, as if to touch her, to embrace her, but then fell back.

"I know your dad loves you," Edward said. "But he might not know how to show it to you. To any of his daughters, for that matter."

"He thinks I'm incompetent."

"You said it yourself. He doesn't understand what you do compared to what he can see in Naomi's and Monica's work. You can't think he doesn't love you."

She shook her head, still muffled by his shoulder. "Today wasn't unusual. I've seen his disappointment time and again."

She wanted her father's approval so much, but Edward wanted to show her how much God the Father loved her. "Your father doesn't understand you, but God does."

It made her cry harder. "God doesn't care about me, either."

He couldn't refute how she was feeling. There was someone after her research, maybe after her life, and then her father's harsh words. *God, why are these things happening to Rachel? Why do You seem so far away from her?*

"I should leave the spa." Her voice sounded harder and more brittle than he'd ever heard her before.

"Why?"

"I can't live up to my father's expectations. And maybe he just doesn't love me as much as he loves Naomi and Monica."

"Stop thinking that," Edward replied.

"It must be true. Why else does he treat me this way? He's never this demanding with Naomi. Although he argues with Monica, he doesn't put her down this way or blame her for things that aren't her fault."

She sat up, turning her face away from him. "I should just go away. I could find a job elsewhere easily—I have great qualifications, and I could do product development for any major corporation in the skin-care industry." Her jaw was set, and the coldness of her words seemed to have frozen her body, too, as she sat stiffly on the bench.

These circumstances and her tense relationship with her father were changing her into someone he didn't know. She was moving further and further away from the warm, quirky Rachel he had come to know in the past year.

He missed her. And he didn't know how to get her back.

"I'll finish this product launch," she said, her mouth almost mulish. "Maybe it'll go so well that he'll finally be happy."

"Why is it so important that he be happy? What

about you? You work your fingers to the bone. Don't you deserve to be happy?"

She paused, and flickered a glance at him. It looked almost guilty. But then she pressed her lips together. "I need to work to get this scar-reduction cream out. It's important to me."

There was something deeper there, something she wasn't telling him. It drove her almost as strongly as her father's approval.

She'd moved away from him, and he wanted to draw her back. But her tight shoulders and straight spine deterred him.

And really, what right did he have to comfort her? They'd been getting closer, but because he had been afraid that she would fail him and hurt him the way his father had, he had withdrawn. In a sense he had abandoned her.

He wrapped her cold hand in his. "Rach, I'm here for you. I want to help you."

Her fingers lay unresisting for a long moment. A moment where his heart pounded slow and loud in his ears.

Then she turned her palm into his, laced her fingers with his.

He squeezed tightly. He would try to understand her relationship with her father. He'd protect her and support her through this.

"Tomorrow," she murmured. "I need your help tomorrow."

"What did you need to do?"

She looked him in the eye, her gaze burning with determination. "I need to confront Gloria Reynolds."

"Ms. Reynolds? The spa client?"

She nodded. "I think she's behind all this, but I don't have any proof aside from something she mentioned to Naomi over a year ago. So I'm going to beard the lion in her den."

SEVEN

Rachel rang the doorbell, and suddenly knew exactly how Naomi must have felt when she visited Gloria Reynolds last year.

The pretentious columns flanking the front door, the clean, white lines of the windows and steps, the sparkling glass in the light above the front door—they all screamed, *My money defines who I am.*

Naomi would have reveled in the chance to barge in, upset that balance of money, power, pretense. And now Rachel did, too, a little.

A Hispanic maid opened the door.

"We've come to speak to Ms. Reynolds," Rachel said. "We're from the Joy Luck Life spa."

The maid let them into the echoing foyer. "Please wait here." She bustled away toward the back of the house.

There were dark shadows cast by the rich furniture, and the sunlight filtering through diamond-paned windows seemed weak and sickly. And Rachel told herself that despite Gloria Reynolds's pompous love for display, she also shouldn't forget that the woman might have tried to have her killed.

Footsteps clacked over the marble floors. Rachel turned to see Gloria approach, looking casually elegant in a pantsuit and mule sandals—and also looking as if she expected them.

She smiled, but it was like a glittering baring of teeth. "Hello, Dr. Grant. What a pleasant surprise." She shook Rachel's hand, and her nails scraped softly at her skin.

Gloria turned to Edward. "You were at the spa yesterday."

"Edward Villa." He gave her a polite nod and took the limp fingers, but he released them as if they were covered with slime.

"Edward is helping me with my next product launch." Rachel blurted it out, not sure what else to say. Naomi would have known exactly how to be smooth and gracious, or Monica would have known how to put Gloria at ease.

She was the absentminded researcher who had entered this pretentious house and had no idea what to say, or how to ask her questions.

"We hope you're feeling better after what happened yesterday." Edward's deep voice rumbled smoothly off the silk-lined walls, imparting just the right amount of concern.

Of course. He had dealt with every type of client imaginable, including several wealthy businesswomen. He probably read Gloria's personality and knew exactly how to speak to her.

"I'm feeling tolerably better," she drawled. "Won't you sit down?" She waved them toward a doorway into a stiff, formal drawing room.

Rachel perched on the edge of a brocade chair, but Edward seemed to relax in his seat without seeming too arrogant.

"The spa has certainly had a great deal of excitement lately." Gloria sank gracefully into a divan across from them. "In fact, wasn't it only a year ago that those unfortunate murders happened?"

Her blue eyes opened wide with shock and innocence, but there was a glint there that seemed to be laughing maliciously at Rachel. It made Rachel stiffen her spine and give a wide, hard smile. "The police did such a wonderful job catching the murderer so efficiently. I'm sure you were relieved the spa didn't have to close its doors."

Gloria's cheek twitched, but she said, "Oh, of course." Her smile seemed to grow feral. "I love all your products, Dr. Grant."

Her tone didn't make it sound like a compliment. "Speaking of products, Naomi mentioned to me that you'd asked her about my diamond-dust cleanser."

The words chased the color from Gloria's cheeks even under her mineral makeup. The pulse beat rapidly at her throat, and her hand reached up to smooth it with slightly shaking fingers. "Why...Naomi has a remarkable memory. I only mentioned it in passing. And that was…I think a year ago."

"I'm curious, Ms. Reynolds, because I never released it as a product. It failed in clinical testing." Rachel pinned her with a hard gaze. "So how did you know about it?"

She was so sure she had her. She wasn't sure if she expected her to break down in a heap of tears and confess all, or perhaps faint in despair at being found out.

She didn't expect Gloria to roll her eyes and laugh softly, as if at herself. "I apologize, Dr. Grant. I'm guilty."

"What?"

"I know you keep your research secret, but I happened to be speaking to the CEO of Palm Diamond Direct sometime last summer."

Rachel's cheeks started to burn.

Gloria met her eyes with cold amusement, as if aware of her embarrassment—and reveling in it. "They mentioned they had just supplied you with some ultrafine diamond dust, apparently for some cleanser you were developing. Well, since my husband is a local diamond distributor, I naturally wanted to speak to you to perhaps wheedle you into buying from us next time." Gloria gave her a look that was meant to be impish, but to Rachel, it had an evil cast to it.

"Oh." She didn't know what else to say. All her suspicions now seemed melodramatic.

Yet despite all that, she couldn't shake the feeling

of menace that emanated from Gloria in subtle hints here and there, in a word, in a tone, in the corner of her smiles.

"When I saw PDD a few months later," Gloria continued, "they mentioned you hadn't reordered more, so I assumed the project had been canceled or something like that." Gloria shrugged daintily. *"C'est la vie."*

Ms. Reynolds's gaze narrowed sharply. "Did you come all this way to ask me about it? Am I under suspicion for something *again?*"

The way she said it made Rachel want to sink in her chair. Naomi had suspected Gloria of the murders last year, and now this year, Rachel had showed up and accused her of…what? Knowing about an abandoned project? What was Rachel doing?

But Gloria wasn't done. "I must protest. The Joy Luck Life spa has been incredibly suspicious and rude to a longtime patron. Well, no more." Gloria rose to her feet, all stately indignation. "I will no longer grace your spa with my patronage."

Rachel rose, also, but her legs shook, and the room began to spin.

Gloria's voice rose. "And you can be sure I will tell all of my acquaintances how abominably I've been treated."

The panic rose in Rachel's chest. What had she done? Naomi would kill her. Her father would be livid.

"You may leave now, Dr. Grant." Gloria stared

down her nose at Rachel, and her eyes seemed to be filled with hate.

Edward's hand at her elbow kept her from drowning in that awful gaze. "Let's go, Rachel."

She stumbled out of the house with him. "I feel so stupid."

"No, don't be."

"But it was such a simple explanation…"

Edward paused, looking back at the grand facade to the house. "There's something not right."

"What do you mean?"

"Something about what she said."

Rachel shook her head. "I should have realized that since her husband is in the diamond business, of course she'd speak to other suppliers and stores, of course she might chat with PDD and hear about my diamond-dust order. And the chatty sales rep I talked to mentioned how she couldn't imagine using the dust for anything except cleanser. I didn't say anything to deny or refute it, but really, what else could a dermatologist use it for?"

Edward tucked her into the passenger seat of his truck. "No, you're right, that all seemed logical when she said it, but…"

"But?"

He gripped her hand. "I don't trust her, Rach. Despite everything, I think she's hiding something."

Rachel tried to pray, but her heart wasn't in it. More, her faith wasn't in it.

She stared at her Bible, open on her desk. Sure, she'd had troubles before—like the fiasco with Avignon spa—but she'd always been able to just work harder, come up with more ideas, spend more time at the lab, push herself more.

She had never before felt as if God had it in for her.

No, wasn't that being overly dramatic? After all, the data stolen was two years old, and Naomi had laughed off Gloria's pronouncement of not coming to the spa again with the remark that Gloria had made that pronouncement dozens of times before, usually in response to some scheduling mistake or miscommunication, and more recently after Naomi had visited her last year to question her about the two murders that had happened at the spa. Yet Gloria always came back after a few days. There was also the fact that Gloria's very expensive Tamarind membership fee, which allowed her use of the exclusive Tamarind lounge and special services at the spa, was already paid up for the year, and despite her wealth, Gloria's actions were often excessively miserly.

But the sabotaged plants, Steve Schmidt's deceit, her ransacked bedroom… Once again, the feeling of being overwhelmed sank upon her mind.

Why were all these things happening? Why was *God* allowing all these things to happen?

She was a good Christian girl. She went to church every week—well, unless she had an experiment. She didn't read her Bible as often as she should, but she tried to read it at least once a week.

Unlike Aunt Becca, Rachel had never felt as if God were present in a room with her—although as a child she had pictured Jesus a bit like an invisible best friend—but now, she felt horribly alone. Abandoned. God was not there for her.

And now, she wondered if He ever had been.

No, she couldn't think like that. After years of being a Christian, was she going to throw it all away because of hardships worse than normal? She had never given up so easily on her work—why would she do so with her faith?

She gave up trying to pray, and picked up her Bible. Over the past year, she'd been going through the entire Bible and was finally in Revelation.

But the words swam in front of her eyes with chemical formulas. What exactly had been stolen? She should do an exhaustive search to figure it out.

After she read her Bible.

But the worry kept intruding, and her reading was more like just going through the motions. Finally, she closed her Bible. The passage was one that didn't make sense to her anyway—something about luke-warm water and God spitting it out of His mouth.

First, she got on her computer and checked her research calendar to see what projects had been at the forefront at the time of the computer hack. Yep, it was all there—on the day of the hack, she had scheduled herself for one more "vehicle" experiment, or one more shot at perfecting the properties of the cleanser paste itself so that it would soften the harsher effects of the diamond dust added to it.

At the time, she'd suspected the diamond-dust cleanser would be a bust, so she'd also been looking into other potential research ideas. She had scheduled action items like a phone call with another researcher—there had been brief talks about a collaboration for a wrinkle cream that never panned out—and also a note to read up on a few saved articles about hand creams.

Rachel searched the weeks before, but she hadn't specifically scheduled anything to do with the scar-reduction cream. She hadn't begun working on that project until several months after Steve Schmidt had been fired.

She frowned as she stared at her calendar. She could have sworn she started working on the scar-reduction cream sooner than that.

She did a search for *Ocimum Redemptiorum,* the basil species name, but only came up with all her experiment reports and protocols, and none of them dated before the blue-coded dates on her calendar, which were after the date of the hack.

But she knew she had some preliminary notes on the project before she actually drew up protocols and started experiments. She opened a master document with her notations on the scar-reduction cream, but none were dated. When did she make these? How to search her computer for the dates?

She called Jane. "Hi, it's Rachel."

"Everything okay with your computer?"

"Yes…well, I'm at a loss."

"What do you need?"

"How can I figure out exactly when I made certain notes in my files?"

"You mean, you have the current versions, but you want to know what was in the older versions of the file when your computer was hacked."

"Yes, exactly."

"Oh, that's easy. Just search through your backup drive."

She had a backup drive?

It sounded as if Jane stifled a giggle. "You forgot about it, didn't you?"

"Did you tell me about it?"

"Of course I did. I told you at the same time I explained the security firewall I installed for your system when I set it all up."

"Oh, but that was years ago—"

"And I tell you again every quarter when I upgrade your security system."

Busted. "Tell me again?"

Jane walked her through how to access her external backup drive, which she discovered was the cute little box sitting under her desk, nestled inconspicuously in all the wires running to and fro.

"You should see a list of folders on your computer screen," Jane said.

"But these aren't old, some of these are new folders."

"If you go to the top right, there should be a scroll bar."

"Okay."

"Click on the bar and pick a date."

She did, and some folders disappeared. "What happened?"

"What's in the window should be the old versions of everything that was on your computer on that date."

"Oh, okay. But the notes on the basil plant could be in one of several files. Do I have to just open them all and search through them?"

"No, there's an easier way. You can input the basil plant name in the data field in the top right corner of the window. Do you see it?"

"Yes." She typed in the basil name.

"Now click the search button, and it will find that name only among the files from that backup date."

Oh, that was convenient. She got a window that said, "No results." Suddenly, it was as if a woolly lining had been cleared from her lungs, and she could breathe easier. "Hooray! Jane, it says 'no results.'"

"Great, that means you didn't write any notes about the basil plant on that day."

"Do I have to search through each backup date to find when I first took notes on the basil?"

"No, there's a special search function I set up." Jane gave a series of instructions and Rachel inputted her basil-plant search term.

"What does the window say?"

"It gives me a listing of folders."

"At the top of the window is a date column. Click that to list the folders by date."

She did. "The oldest date is a few weeks after Steve left." But the date was also a few months earlier than when the item showed up blue-coded on her calendar, so this was a more accurate record of when she started working on it.

"When does this backup occur?"

"Every evening at eleven. So the folder for the day of the hack will include exactly the files he stole, unless you added more to the notes after you discovered Steve in the lab that night."

"No, I fired him that night and watched him clean out his desk, then I went back home."

"Okay, well, you're set then?"

"Yes, thanks, Jane." Rachel disconnected the call.

She opened the oldest file that referenced the basil plant and read her notes.

Ocimum Redemptiorum: Sickly growth. Find expert in growing tropical plants for advice. Must also arrange for possible mass production.

Preliminary formulation notes…

Wait a minute. These phrases seemed to indicate this wasn't the first time she was taking notes on this plant. Rachel went back to the window and clicked the date column again, but this file came up as the oldest one.

She redid the search with the basil name, but came up with the same results.

An ache like heartburn started in her chest, and she rubbed it. She must have begun work on the plant before this date. But when? And why couldn't she find it when searching for the basil name?

Wait, she had gotten the basil seeds from Aunt Becca's friend, Ellen, who had been a missionary in Malaysia for several years. Ellen had noticed villagers rubbing the basil leaves on scars and had witnessed its ability to reduce them, and so she had contacted Aunt Becca and Rachel, sending the seeds for her to grow and eventually experiment on.

Rachel searched for Ellen's name, but all that came up were some old e-mails she had saved when the missionary had first contacted her. The basil plant name wasn't even mentioned. The e-mails, however, were dated before Steve was fired. Had she begun to experiment on the plant and develop the formula when he'd been fired, or had she only been growing the basil?

Rachel searched for Malaysia and found some notes she'd taken when she'd had several phone calls with Ellen later to discuss the plant, but Rachel hadn't recorded the calls, only taken notes. The calls took place before Steve was fired, but the notes didn't seem to indicate she had started formulation yet.

However, they also didn't give her a clue as to when she did start formulation—whether before or after the computer hack.

She did a few more searches using fragments of the chemical formula as search terms, but came up with absolutely nothing. Apparently there were limitations to Jane's search engine.

When had she started formulation? Had Steve been able to steal the basil formula?

She sat back in her chair. All this still didn't make sense. Even if Steve had stolen the formula, why did they steal the basil plants from the greenhouse?

Or maybe Edward was mistaken, and there weren't any plants missing after all....

A sharp metallic rattle cut through the quiet of the lab.

Rachel twisted in her chair, her heart knocking around in her chest as she stared out her open office door at the darkened lab.

The sound had come from the locked doors to the lab area. Someone had shaken the push bar on the outside to try to open the heavy door, but the steel double bolts hadn't been disengaged—that only happened when someone swiped a card key and inputted a numeric code on the touch pad.

Rachel stood up slowly. Maybe she'd been imagining things. She crept softly out of her office and approached the double doors. There was a narrow vertical crack of light between them from the outside hallway.

A shadow cut the beam.

She clapped a hand to her mouth to keep herself from screaming.

Scrabbling sounded outside in the hallway, as if someone were wrestling with the card-key-code pad on the wall. Again, someone loudly jammed against the door. Rachel jumped. Thankfully, the door held.

It better—her father had spared no expense to guard the laboratory area at the rear of the spa building.

Rachel hurried back to her office. Maybe she was blowing this out of proportion. Maybe it was just one of the security guards. They made walk-throughs of the building every few hours, and that included the lab area. In fact, that had been how they'd caught Steve Schmidt in the lab with his girlfriend that night.

She dialed the security guards' desk. The phone rang. And rang. And rang.

No one picked up.

There were two guards these days—implemented after the murders at the spa the year before. One of them should have picked up.

She tried again. Whoever was outside the lab jammed against the door once more, making her drop the phone. She fumbled to pick it up, but it still rang. Neither of the guards answered her call.

She hung up the phone, her hands trembling. If a guard was trying to get in he had card-key access to the lab. There was no reason he'd be locked out.

If Rachel tried to run, there was only one door into the lab area. The only other exit was an emergency window exit, which when opened would activate an alarm and automatically call both the fire department and police department.

Except the emergency exit was fifty yards from her office, at the very back of the lab.

No, she should lock herself in her office, thankful for the newly installed dead bolt on the door. And call someone.

She shut her office door as quietly as she could and turned off the lights, in hopes that whoever was out there didn't realize she had arrived early at the spa to do some work. Edward hadn't been happy to drive her so early, but he had already been awake—the drive had only cut into his morning coffee time.

So she knew he would be awake. He could make it to the spa within a few minutes.

Faster than any police cars.

She punched in his number on her cell phone, and he picked up on the first ring. "Rachel?"

"Edward, come quick!" she whispered just as the doors were jiggled again.

"What's that sound?" he asked sharply. "What's wrong?" She heard his car keys clinking.

"Someone's trying to get in through the card-key doors to the lab. I can't get hold of any of the guards."

"I'm on my—"

His words were cut off by the unmistakable snap of the lab-door dead bolts being disengaged. Rachel shot off her chair and crouched in the corner of her office. "He's inside," she told Edward softly.

What could she do? How long would the dead bolt last on her office door? She dimly heard Edward shouting into the phone, but it was hard to hear him because of the dull roar in her ears.

"Rachel, stay put! I'm on—"

"Dr. Grant?"

Martin. The spa security guard's voice filtered through her overwrought senses. She stood up slowly, still silent. What if he wasn't alone? What if an intruder was forcing him at gunpoint?

"Dr. Grant, are you okay?" A soft knocking on her office door. Martin's voice didn't sound strained or under duress.

Heat radiated from her neck and cheeks. Had she been overreacting? She flicked on her office lights, unbolted the door and peeked out.

Martin smiled at her. "Taking a nap? You need it."

She smiled weakly.

"You shouldn't be working late and then coming in so early, Dr. Grant." He had the chiding voice of an uncle—and after working for the Grants for so many years, he often treated Naomi and Rachel like his own daughters.

She cleared her throat, which had closed up tight while she'd been scared out of her mind. "I just tried calling the security desk, but no one answered."

"Andrew is clearing the lens on an outside camera.

We noticed there was something splattered on the picture we saw in the video monitors." Martin began walking through the darkened lab, doing a cursory sweep. "I had to do my walk-through, though, so I left the security desk." He glanced at her. "Should I have stayed to watch the monitors? I figured since Andrew was outside…"

"That's fine, Martin."

He shook his head. "No, I probably should have stayed at the desk. Andrew can't see on the other side of the building. I'll go back now." He headed toward the door, then paused. "Oh, and you should know that ever since that man tampered with the card-key pad, it's been acting up. I had a hard time getting into the lab just now—had to run my card and input my code several times before it let me in." He left the lab.

Rachel wanted to sink through the floor.

Then she remembered she'd been on the phone with Edward. She lifted the cell phone to her ear. "Edward—"

"I heard."

"I'm sorry for alarming you," she said in a small voice. "I really thought someone was trying to break into the lab."

"All things considered, it's probably best for you to be paranoid rather than sorry."

His approval was like a comforting hot water bottle laid against her stomach, relaxing the taut muscles.

Her father would have been annoyed and

blamed her for being silly. Edward, however, understood her.

It was a surprising feeling to Rachel. Different. Something she hadn't felt since her mother died.

"I'll let you get back to work." Her voice came out a bit thick. She cleared her throat. "Thanks."

"I'll pick you up tonight." He clicked off.

Another sharp jiggle of the lab door made her start. She almost went to open the door for whoever it was, thinking it might be Martin again, but then Edward's words stopped her—better to be paranoid than sorry.

She remembered the car hitting her bike, and shuddered.

She hid behind her office door frame and stared intently at the lab double doors. Whoever it was scrabbled at the card-key pad.

The door bolts disengaged.

She held her breath.

"Hi, Dr. Grant." Stephanie, her research associate, gave her a casual glance as she flicked on the general lab lights and removed a fuzzy light blue knitted scarf.

Rachel took a steadying breath before she answered. Too much excitement for this early in the morning. "You're in early today."

"I needed to talk to you," Stephanie said, her mouth grim.

Was she quitting? Rachel tried to hide her inward tension. She hated hiring new lab assistants.

Stephanie took a few steps toward her office and stopped, chewing on her lip and staring at the floor. "I'm not sure how to tell you this."

"What is it? Just spit it out. Don't worry."

Stephanie looked up at her, hazel eyes wide. "Someone called me last night, Dr. Grant."

"A headhunter?" Rachel wondered which lab enticed Stephanie away from her. She had thought Stephanie had been glad to get a research job so close to her parents' home in Santa Rosa, but maybe she was wrong.

"No, not a headhunter." Stephanie swallowed. "Dr. Grant, a man promised me $100,000 if I would steal your scar-reduction-cream formula from you."

EIGHT

"She could be lying." Edward took another sip of coffee while keeping an eye on Rachel, who was nursing a cup of green tea.

Augustus took a sip of his own tea, then frowned down at his cup. "If that's so, what would be the reason?"

"She's not lying." Rachel tucked a dark strand of hair behind her ear, a nervous gesture. What was making her uncomfortable? Her father? Him? Or maybe she was just on edge because of everything happening?

Then again, she'd been very quiet the entire drive home tonight. But she'd invited him inside to discuss Stephanie's confession with her father. If it was his presence making her nervous, he wasn't sure if that made him happy or upset.

"How long has Stephanie been working for you?" Augustus asked.

"Two years."

"She hasn't given you any problems?"

"None, Dad." There was a soft edge to her tone, as

if she didn't appreciate the implication that she'd hired another "trouble" employee. Edward remembered the overheard argument, and guessed that father and daughter hadn't spoken about it to each other since.

"Stephanie was in Alex's grade in school," Edward said, his voice cutting through the rather sharp looks exchanged between Rachel and Augustus. "She was smart and friendly. And she always seemed a bit ambitious."

Rachel's eyebrows rose. "Really? When I hired her, she said she'd been hoping for a research job close to her parents and that the spa job was perfect. There aren't many chemistry research labs in this area."

Edward shrugged. "Maybe her years in college changed her." He thought a moment. "Or maybe she's the same."

"What do you mean?" Augustus and Rachel asked at the same time, in exactly the same tone. They looked at each other, then looked away.

"What if she's telling the truth, but she didn't refuse the man like she told you she did?"

Rachel's brow furrowed. "But if she told the man she'd steal my formula, why bother to tell me?"

"I think I know," Augustus said slowly. "It's what I'd do if I were in her position and wanted the money. I'd tell you in order to 'prove' my loyalty to you."

Edward nodded. "She'd be more likely to be retained as a 'trustworthy' research assistant, giving her a chance to steal the formulation."

"The man just talked to her yesterday—"

"That's what she told you," Edward said. "What if it was last week, and she's already had a chance to try to get the formulation but failed?"

"We only recently installed the dead bolt to your office door," Augustus said. "It makes it harder to get to your computer. She'd have to get your key, or you'd have to be in the spa but have left your office door open."

Rachel's cheeks burned red. "I don't do that, ever, Dad. I know how important my research is."

"She'd also need you to be logged in to your computer to download anything," Edward said. "Your cousin made a good security system for you."

"It would help her if you thought she was faithful to you," Augustus said.

Rachel shook her head. "I don't like this. This is just speculation. We're judging the poor girl without knowing the truth."

"You should protect yourself and just let her go," Augustus said bluntly.

Rachel's face drained of color. "Dad!"

Edward had to admit he saw the logic of the suggestion, but it pained him to think of committing a drastic move like that against someone just because circumstances were suspicious.

"If Stephanie is being honest, how would it repay her to fire her?" Rachel demanded.

"If she's not being honest, then you're taking yourself out of harm's way," Augustus argued.

"I may be taking the research out of harm's way, but I'd be a poor excuse for a human being."

"Is Stephanie your only lab employee?" Edward asked.

Rachel nodded, her eyes wary.

Edward read her look—she wasn't sure if he was her ally or not. He didn't want to take sides, but he did want to smooth things between the two Grants. "How about putting the lab on temporary shutdown?"

Rachel's mouth opened in a small *O*. Then she smiled, and it was more beautiful than a Lady Slipper orchid.

"That's a wonderful idea," she said.

"How long?" demanded Augustus. "Until we discover who's doing all this? That could take weeks." He had said it himself—he understood the bottom line, and the word shutdown usually meant losing money.

"It wouldn't be a true shutdown," Edward said. "Since Stephanie's her only employee, Rachel can continue to work, but Stephanie won't be able to get into the lab to steal anything."

"But officially, she'd still be an employee. I wouldn't have to fire her," Rachel said.

Augustus still frowned. "I don't like paying someone to not do any work."

"She'll make up for it, Dad. She's on salary, not hourly." Rachel pointed to the calendar on his desk. "She'll put in her hours when it's time to mass produce the scar-reduction cream. Both she and I will be busy soon since we're still committed to releasing the cream in the spring." But there was a strain around her eyes as she said it.

Augustus didn't seem to notice. He grunted and nodded.

Edward could see that despite her words, she believed this shutdown *would* affect her product launch. And she wasn't just concerned or alarmed or stressed.

She was afraid.

Rachel checked the clock while trying to sift through the clinical data on her computer screen, but she couldn't do both at once. And each time she saw the time advance, the knot in her stomach drew itself tighter and tighter.

Almost quitting time. Almost time to tell Stephanie the bad news.

No, it wasn't bad news. She wasn't firing her research associate. Stephanie would be paid during the shutdown—she would probably be thrilled.

Or Stephanie would guess the real reason for the shutdown and feel hurt and betrayed after confessing all to Rachel the morning before.

But it wasn't just telling her research assistant—Rachel had also arranged for Detective Carter to arrive to question her about the man. She figured Stephanie wouldn't mind, since the girl had immediately and fully confessed what the man had asked her to do.

Maybe Rachel should make sure Detective Carter was coming. She abandoned her clinical-trial numbers and picked up her cell phone, although a cowardly *meow* sounded in her mind.

She was only putting off the inevitable.

She put the phone down.

Standing up, she straightened her blouse, her hair and her spine. She marched out of her office into the lab area.

"Hey, Dr. Grant. I was just finishing up." Stephanie glanced at her from where she was cleaning up some data on her computer. "Give me a sec and I'll e-mail these results to you."

"Thanks, Stephanie." Rachel's stiff backbone sagged a little. No use interrupting her data crunching, after all….

"There, I just sent it to you." Stephanie turned in her chair to smile at her. "I wasn't sure I'd get it done by the end of today."

Rachel tried to smile, but her jaw was made of gelatin. "Stephanie, I have some bad—er, good news."

Her research assistant had a deer-in-the-headlights look. Something about it put Rachel on edge—but then again, she was already on edge because of what she had to tell her.

"You're not going to fire me, are you?"

"No! Not at all," Rachel hastened to assure her.

Stephanie relaxed a fraction, but there was still a tenseness about her face—not just the tension of anticipating bad news, but a strange tenseness Rachel couldn't interpret.

Rachel plunged ahead. "It will actually make you happy. My dad—I mean, *I* have decided that with everything that has happened lately against the lab, it would be best to shut it down for a few weeks until the police figure out what's going on."

"Shut down the lab?" Stephanie's voice rose a notch.

"You'll be paid," Rachel interjected. "It'll be paid leave for you."

"I'm not..." Stephanie swallowed. "I'm not being fired, am I?"

"No, don't worry, you're not being fired."

Stephanie's expression was still troubled.

"You're one of the best research assistants I've had," Rachel added. "I wouldn't want to lose you."

Somehow, her reassurance only made Stephanie look down into her lap. "But I...I told you about that man."

Rachel felt sick. "I'm not punishing you for being honest."

"It just feels that way." Stephanie looked ten years younger, small and hurt.

"I'm sorry, Stephanie. It's just that the police are concerned about the attempts against the lab. In fact, Detective Carter is on his way. He wants to ask you about the man who tried to bribe you."

Stephanie's alarmed eyes darted first to Rachel, then to the lab door. "Detective Carter?"

"You're not in trouble, Stephanie. After all, you didn't receive any money from him, did you?"

"No, no," she quickly said. "He just offered me the money if I would steal your formula, he didn't give me any." She breathed deeply. "It just frightened me a little because it's so...*official*. I've never even gotten a parking ticket."

"I can understand that." Rachel remembered her trepidation the first time she got a speeding ticket.

The bolts on the lab doors clicked, and the doors swung open. Detective Carter entered with a nod to Martin, who had accessed the lab for him.

After Rachel made the introductions, Detective Carter took out his notebook and asked, "So this man called you out of the blue?"

"Yes. He offered me the money to steal Dr. Grant's formula, but I hung up on him."

"And when was this?"

"The day before yesterday."

"He only called you the one time?"

Stephanie blinked rapidly, then her brow furrowed. "Actually, I think he called a few other times before that, but my mom answered my phone line at home. She mentioned talking to a strange man who wouldn't leave his name."

The detective noted it down. "We'll look into your phone records to find out what number he's calling from."

Stephanie nodded, biting her lip.

"Did you ever meet him in person?"

She shook her head.

"He never mentioned how he got your telephone number?"

"No."

"Can you describe his voice?"

Stephanie looked at a loss, and shrugged a few times. "I don't know...deep enough that I knew it was a man." Her gaze flickered to Rachel. "I'm sorry I can't give a better description."

"No, that's fine," Detective Carter said.

"Voices are hard to describe," Rachel added.

Rachel's gut relaxed as the detective finished up with Stephanie. That had been painful but not too bad. And she was very glad that was over with.

After Detective Carter left, Stephanie gave Rachel a soft "Goodbye" as she collected her purse and car keys. She gave her a brief look—hurt, concerned and still tense from the conversation with the detective—before heading out the door.

That one quick look hovered in front of Rachel's eyes as she finished up her clinical-trial data crunching and packed up for the day.

She met Aunt Becca in the spacious entrance foyer to the spa. "I'm going to call Edward, Aunt Becca."

Her aunt placed a warm hand on her arm. "I talked to Horatio before he left. He said Stephanie was as helpful as she could be."

Rachel nodded. "It scared her to talk to a policeman. I think she wondered if she had done anything wrong."

"She's a sweet girl."

"She was really hurt by the news about the lab shutdown." Rachel chewed on her bottom lip.

"Well, I don't really blame her, but you don't have much of a choice." Aunt Becca gave her a quick hug. "Don't worry too much about it. You did the right thing."

"I'm going to leave early. That confrontation left me feeling like a rag doll."

"The lab's locked up? Stephanie already left through the staff entrance in back?"

Rachel nodded. "I'm sorry to leave you here to run the spa by yourself tonight."

Aunt Becca waved it aside. "I'm spa hostess. It's my job. Besides, it's nearly seven o'clock, so it's only for a couple more hours."

"I wonder what Naomi did with Devon in San Francisco today."

"Had too much fun." Aunt Becca winked at her. "They don't get to spend time together often enough. I hope they get married soon."

Suddenly, the front doors *whooshed* open and Naomi rushed into the entrance foyer, followed by Devon Knightley. Her tense face took in the two receptionists at the desk, and she slowed her steps slightly, but her wide eyes gave an unspoken plea to her sister and aunt.

"Naomi," Rachel said, a question in her tone.

"Hi, Ms. Grant," chimed the two receptionists,

although their glances to Naomi and Devon were curious.

"Hi, girls. I'll be in my office," Naomi told them, and Rachel, Aunt Becca and Devon followed her rapid steps. Devon shut her office door behind them as Naomi dropped her laptop bag on her desk.

"You're back early," Rachel started to say, then noticed the bruise on Naomi's wrist. "Where in the world did you get that?"

"Naomi," exclaimed Aunt Becca, reaching out to grasp her wrist.

"I'm fine," Naomi said.

"That doesn't look fine," Aunt Becca retorted.

"Ask Devon." Naomi nodded at him.

Dr. Knightley placed a hand on Aunt Becca's shoulder. "It looks worse than it is."

"It looks awful," Rachel blurted out. Black, purple and red bloomed on her sister's skin in a shape that looked like a large hand had grabbed her.

"What happened?" demanded Aunt Becca.

"I was attacked in San Francisco."

Aunt Becca gasped. Rachel's chest tightened. "Attacked? Why? How?"

"It was right outside my office," said Devon. "I was only a few feet behind her."

"My laptop was strung over my shoulder." Naomi pointed to the laptop bag on the desk. "I had just exited Devon's office when I felt someone yank at it. Well, I yanked back." The look in her eyes was fierce enough to frighten off any assailant.

"Actually, the laptop would have been stolen if your sister weren't so strong," Devon said.

"Yes, well, I'm not a massage therapist for nothing."

"Someone tried to steal your laptop? Again?" Rachel was incredulous. "What are the odds?"

"No, here's what's weird." Naomi leaned in toward her. "The man trying to take it grabbed my wrist—that's how I got the bruise—and then he looked up at me. And he hesitated. Rach, he was *surprised*."

"Surprised?"

"And so I grabbed him," Devon said.

"He let go of my wrist, and I grabbed the laptop back," Naomi said. "And then I got a good look at him." Naomi reached out to grip Rachel's shoulder. "Rach, it was the same man who tried to get into the labs the other day."

NINE

Edward thought he saw pleasure in Rachel's eyes when she saw him enter the spa with Detective Carter. "You're here early. I had been about to call you," she said.

"Horatio was talking to Alex when you called, so I tagged along." He nodded toward where the detective had gone to speak to Becca. "Twice in one day, huh?"

Rachel gave him a rueful look. "Poor man. He's tired of our demanding family."

"You need to stop having crimes at the spa," Edward said.

"This time it wasn't at the spa, but it did involve a Grant."

Horatio approached Naomi. "Let's go to your office and you can tell me what happened," he said.

They all trooped back into Naomi's office, and she talked about the man grabbing her laptop and hesitating.

"He looked surprised?" Edward asked. "Are you sure?"

Naomi nodded.

"Surprised at what?"

"He looked surprised at Naomi," Devon said.

"As if he was expecting someone else?" Edward asked. "As if he were expecting to see *Rachel?*"

Silence for a brief moment, during which Rachel's face paled and the pulse in her throat picked up its pace.

"Rach was carrying the laptop when it was first stolen," Naomi said.

"And I was with you when you bought it earlier that day," Rachel added. "They might have thought the laptop was mine...if someone were watching us." She shivered.

"But it was new, so it didn't have any information on it," Naomi said. "And they returned it."

"With that bogus note," Becca said bitterly. "And I told you not to call the police. I'm such an old fool."

"Aunt Becca, we all thought it was a wayward teen," Rachel said.

"So they returned the laptop and gave you a week or so to load more information on it," said Devon. "Then tried to take it again. But when the man saw Naomi, he was surprised because he'd thought the laptop was Rachel's."

Edward stared hard at the laptop case on Naomi's desk. "But how did he know you'd be in San Francisco today? Especially if he thought the computer was Rachel's?" He unzipped the case and removed the computer.

"You're not going to take it apart, are you?" Becca asked.

"No, I wouldn't dare. Although if you want Alex to do it…"

"I might," Naomi said, ignoring Becca's head shake.

Edward searched the case. It was a simple padded case, made of tough, cheap canvas and synthetic materials. When the laptop had been returned, he hadn't thought to examine the case closely. After all, they'd thought it had been a kid forced to return it.

He looked to Naomi. "Do you have a utility knife?"

She nodded and rummaged in her desk drawer.

"Shouldn't Horatio do that?" Becca asked.

"Go ahead, Edward," the detective said.

Edward took the utility knife and gently ripped open the seams of the laptop case. He pulled out the polyester stuffing carefully, followed by the foam padding.

And then he saw it.

A small electronic device. Alex could have probably identified it easily. And it definitely did not belong in the laptop case, hidden among the stuffing.

"What is that?" Rachel peered at it as Edward laid it on Naomi's desk.

"A GPS tracker?" Devon guessed. "That's how they knew the laptop would be in San Francisco."

"But not that it would be Naomi carrying it and not Rachel," Edward finished.

Horatio looked at Devon. "Did the man have anyone else with him?"

"After I tackled him and he let go of Naomi, he took off. I chased him, but he got into the passenger side of a car waiting on the other side of the street. The car took off pretty fast, so he at least had another person driving for him."

"Did you get a license plate?"

"No."

"Make and model?"

Devon glanced at Rachel. "Blue Ford Taurus."

Edward had been expecting the answer, but it still made him clench his teeth.

"We filed a complaint with the San Francisco police," Naomi said. "We also told them about the man trying to get into the labs, and we told them to speak to you about the outside video-surveillance tapes we gave to you."

"I looked at the tapes," Horatio said. "They didn't get a good picture of the man. He deliberately kept his head down. But we have a description of his height and weight."

Rachel was still staring at the electronic device. "They wanted the laptop because they wanted my formula," she said softly.

"You've taken precautions to protect your lab and computer, Dr. Grant?" asked Horatio.

She nodded. "My cousin Jane looked over my computer a few days ago, and I have a new lock on my office door."

"But we need to fix the card-key lock to the lab," Becca said.

Edward frowned. "The lab door lock is broken?"

"Not broken," Rachel said. "The man who tried to get in tampered with the card-key pad and now sometimes it takes a few tries before the door unlocks."

"I would suggest you take care of that as soon as possible," Horatio said. "These people are getting bolder. They've shown their faces—this one man, at least—and they've escalated to attacking you in broad daylight."

"What will they try to do next?" Becca cried. She placed her arms around Rachel, her face crumpled in fear for her niece.

"We'll get him," Horatio promised, his voice growling in conviction. Detective Carter typically had a mild demeanor, but his steely eyes always reminded Edward that he could be very dangerous, which made him a good cop.

But Rachel turned a sober expression to the detective. Edward couldn't blame her—Horatio's determination alone couldn't protect her.

So Edward would try to take up the slack.

Their relationship was undefined at this point, and he still wasn't sure about her faith, but he couldn't fight the need to help her anymore than he could fight gravity. He'd sort out his feelings later, at a more quiet moment. Right now, the danger seemed to be circling closer and faster.

Rachel's lips thinned as she stared at the shredded

laptop case, the electronic device that Detective Carter was even now storing away in an evidence bag. At the same time, her hands and shoulders shook, and she clenched her arms around herself as if to keep from flying apart.

"Come on," Becca said, tugging at her arm. "Let's get you home."

"No." She said it quietly, but with a thread of steel that somehow reminded Edward of her father.

Becca tilted her head. "Rachel, you're exhausted. We all are. Let's go home, get some dinner—"

"No, I can't." She lifted her chin as she faced her aunt. "I can't do anything about this, but I can at least devote more time and energy to figuring out exactly what information they did steal from my computer."

Naomi shook her head. "Rach, it's late."

But Rachel was shaking her head, too. "I've been going through the archived files slowly, but after this attack on you…" Her shoulders heaved once. Twice. "I haven't been spending enough time going through those files. I have to do a more exhaustive search— and the sooner, the better."

Becca gave Edward a worried glance. "But Edward will have to wait, too."

Rachel turned to him. "Why don't you go home, and I'll call you when I need a ride? Or if it's late, I can ask one of the security guards to drive me."

"No," he insisted. "No matter what time it is, call me."

"Are you sure?"

"Yes." He would be there for her. And maybe make up for the time he had spent trying to stay aloof from her. He hadn't understood her at all.

"I have to do this, Aunt Becca." Rachel took her aunt's hand. "I have to. I need to keep busy."

Becca's mouth opened and closed silently, but Naomi seemed to understand, and she gently steered her aunt out of the office. "Devon and I will take you home, Aunt Becca. It's almost time for the spa to close, anyway."

"It's actually a good thing I've shut down the lab," Rachel said to Edward as the detective followed them into the hallway.

"Aside from the question about Stephanie's innocence?" Edward asked.

"It gives me time to search my files. I'm determined, Edward." Her eyes were fierce. "Thirty-six hours from now, I'm determined to know exactly what Steve stole from my computer. It's got to be more than just the defunct diamond-dust project."

At thirty-seven hours and twelve minutes, she still hadn't figured it out.

She'd stayed at the lab around the clock, catching a couple hours' rest in a sleeping bag on the floor of her office. She'd read all the archived files of various project notes from the day of the computer hack and found no mention of the basil plant or the scar-reduction-cream formula.

Which she probably should consider a good thing, because it implied that Steve hadn't gotten any information about the project when he stole the files off her computer. But there was still the niggling suspicion that she was missing something. That he had stolen something vital to do with the scar-reduction cream, or else why go through the effort to trash the greenhouse and steal three basil plants? If a rival company were starting from there, they were already too far behind. They must have had a better reason than to play catch-up.

She glanced at the clock, surprised that it was already almost ten o'clock in the morning. She hadn't had more than a cup of coffee since she got up from a short nap around five.

She jolted when her office phone blared. "Hello?"

"Hi, Dr. Grant. It's Stephanie."

"Hi, Stephanie. Is everything okay?" Why would she be calling her?

"Everything's fine. I'm sorry to bother you, but I might have left my cell phone in my desk at work— I've been using Mom's cell phone since I noticed it missing."

"Oh. Did you want me to get it for you?"

"The thing is, I'm not positive I left it there. I've looked everywhere for it, and it's the only place I haven't tried yet."

"Have you tried calling it? I haven't heard it ring."

"I always put it on silent when I do experiments, because I don't want the ringing to distract me if I'm doing some sensitive pipetting."

That's true, and Rachel appreciated Stephanie's conscientiousness about her work performance. "Stephanie, I have the lab on shutdown."

"I know, and I'm sorry to have to ask you, but would you be able to let me in to look?"

Rachel didn't want to do it. But how to tell Stephanie without being outright mean and suspicious?

"I promise, Dr. Grant, you won't even need to come out of your office. If you have the security guards open the card-key door for me, I'll look through my desk and then leave."

Rachel didn't really like suspecting Stephanie—after all, the girl had worked for her for two years and had told her about being offered money to steal her formulation. Plus she could just have one of the guards escort Stephanie so she wouldn't be alone in the lab with her. "Okay, I'll tell the guards you're coming by."

"Thanks, Dr. Grant. I'll be there in twenty minutes."

Rachel told Martin about Stephanie's visit and asked him to escort her. Only then could she relax a bit and continue looking through the file currently open.

She must be more tired than she realized—her eyes were wigging out as they stared at the monitor. She closed them tightly, rubbing gently, then opened them

again. No, the screen was still jiggling and flipping files....

Wait. She wasn't seeing things—it really was flipping through files.

Was she being hacked again?

Her heart squeezed painfully in her chest, and at the same time her brain seemed to expand, taking in every file, identifying it as it passed off the screen. Her fingers shook as she dialed Jane's number. "Jane, my computer screen is going crazy."

"Are you sure—"

"And I know it's not because I've been working too hard. I can see my files popping up, one after another."

"Rachel," Jane barked, "remember the shutdown procedure I told you to do?"

"Uh...yes."

"Do it now!"

She did. Striking shortcut keys, unplugging certain cords and wires Jane had labeled especially for her. Every quarter when Jane updated her security system, she had drilled the procedure into Rachel over and over again so that her hands would do things automatically if she ever had to shut down her computer this way.

Adrenaline started to kick in, shaking through her hands, drumming wildly in her heart, sizzling in her veins. How dare someone do this...how dare someone try to invade her research...how dare someone attack her here....

The computer went dead with a protesting cry. "Jane, it's done."

"I'm on my way."

Rachel sagged back in her chair, breathing as heavily as if she'd biked a race. Then she pushed away from the dark monitor. She couldn't look at it. She wanted to rage. She wanted to dissolve into tears.

The office seemed quiet without the computer softly humming in the background. Quiet and dark, since she didn't have any windows to the outside. The sun would be shining fitfully through the late-fall chill in the air, gilding the rosebushes surrounding the spa.

She should go out to the gardens and walk around, clear her head.

No, was she stupid? Someone had broken into her bedroom. Someone had tried to hit her on her bike. She was a target, and targets didn't go roaming around spa gardens, even if it was the middle of the morning.

Plus, she still didn't feel she'd figured out what had been stolen. She must be missing something. But the only way to find out for sure would be to look through all the raw data files she had archived, and while she'd glanced through some of them, to go through them all would take days. Exhausting days.

But days she might have to spend. She didn't know where else to look.

She sighed and spun around in her chair to get the computer monitor out of her field of vision, her eyes

falling on the bookshelf with her lab notebooks lined up in rows.

Of course! She sat up in her chair. Why hadn't she thought of those? She recorded her experiment notes by hand initially, and although she typically typed vital information when she wrote up the final reports on her experiments, sometimes she recorded findings in those books if she did small experiments that she wouldn't write a formal report for or on research projects she hadn't yet committed to pursuing as formal projects.

She fingered through them until she found the one she was working on at the time of Steve's hack, and flipped through the pages.

At the time, she had suspected the diamond-dust cleanser project wasn't going to work out, so she had been doing numerous last-ditch efforts to formulate a carrier lotion. But interspersed with those notes were jotted ideas for other projects she might pick up.

Including one for *Reformorum*. That sounded familiar. There, another notation, along with the word scars.

Then it suddenly hit her. When she'd talked with Aunt Becca's missionary friend in Malaysia, Ellen had mentioned the basil species name *Ocimum Reformorum,* and Rachel had jotted it down. But it wasn't until several weeks later when she had gotten the seeds, grown a couple plants and had them DNA-tested that she realized it had been the wrong spe-

cies name—the plant species was actually *Ocimum Redemptiorum.*

When she searched her computer before, she had used the correct species name—*Redemptiorum*—and found the earliest use of that species name in her notes. But she must have been using the wrong species before that, and maybe she forgot to notate in the files when she discovered the correct one.

She paged through the notebook, paying attention to the dates, finding a few references here and there to the incorrect basil species.

No formulations. No chemical notations.

Just *the wrong basil species name.*

Steve had stolen the wrong basil species name.

So whoever hired Steve Schmidt to hack her computer perhaps *had* seen references to the scar-reduction cream in her files, but the references had probably had the wrong basil plant species. They could have been doing formulation experiments using the wrong strain of basil for several months—perhaps up to two years, since the day they got the illicit information. They must have finally realized that they had the wrong basil species, but instead of giving up on the project, they discovered she was still going forward with the basil plants in Edward's greenhouse. They stole the correct plant from the greenhouse, but they had already lost months of research time with the wrong plant and it would be time-consuming starting over again to develop formulation with the new basil.

That meant they needed her formulation, which she'd perfected over the past two years, in order to launch their own scar cream. That's why they'd been trying to get into the lab. That's why they'd tried hacking into her computer today.

And if they sabotaged her scar-reduction-cream product launch, the market would be open for their own product. That explained the attack on the greenhouse, trying to destroy all her plants.

She sat, staring at the lab notebook, unsure how to feel. On one hand, she ought to be rejoicing because Steve obviously hadn't stolen any formulation information. According to the notebook, she hadn't yet started developing formulas at the time and didn't begin those experiments until several weeks later.

But whoever paid Steve to get the information had found out about her scar-reduction cream and the properties of the basil.

But they'd also had the wrong basil species.

She glanced at the clock. Where was Jane? She wanted to look through her computer for the wrong basil species name to see what references popped up.

She heard the card-key door locks disengage.

"Hi, Dr. Grant," Martin called to her.

"I'll just be a second," Stephanie said.

That's right, Stephanie had said she was coming by. Rachel heard the sounds of Stephanie rummaging through her metal lab-desk drawers. Then soft footsteps approaching her office and a soft tap on her office door.

"Dr. Grant? I found my cell phone. Thanks. Um… can I talk to you for just a second?"

Her voice sounded edgy, wavering. Rachel sat still for a moment. No, she shouldn't let her in.

But Martin was with her. And Rachel's computer was shut down—no one could pull any information off it until Jane got here, and that would be any moment now.

She unlocked the door and opened it a crack, her heart racing. "I'm a bit busy, Stephanie." She saw Martin's form a few feet behind the research assistant, watchful but trying not to be intrusive.

The girl bit her lip, her eyes darting up to Rachel's face, then down to the cell phone in her hand. Her other hand fingered the smooth fabric of her jacket.

The nervous gestures caused alarm bells clanging through Rachel's head. She placed a hand against the door to slam it shut, but Stephanie blurted out, "I got another job offer."

It seemed that getting out the words released her pent-up energy. Stephanie's face smoothed, and excitement glimmered in her eyes and her smile.

"Another job?"

"It was such a fluke, Dr. Grant. My old research supervisor has been working for her brother's biotech start-up company for a few years, and they just got another round of funding, so she got the go-ahead to hire more people, and she wants to pull me into the company while it's still taking off, and it's in San Francisco and it starts in two weeks and it's doing all

the biochemistry stuff I love doing and…" Stephanie's face fell a little. "I'm so sorry, Dr. Grant. I know it's a pain to have to hire someone else so close to your product launch."

"No, I'm very happy for you, Stephanie." And she was—happy that her suspicions about Stephanie were obviously unfounded. She'd find another research associate—she didn't want to think about that now. There were too many other things to worry about.

Stephanie smiled and heaved a sigh. "I was so nervous about telling you," she confessed. "I'm sorry to leave you in the lurch like this, but it's a great opportunity."

"Of course you can't pass this up," Rachel said. "I wish you only the best."

"Thanks, Dr. Grant." Stephanie held out her hand. "I appreciate it. It's been great working for you."

Rachel shook the girl's hand.

Stephanie smiled and turned away, but she turned quickly in a wide circle as if going back into the lab area, bumping into Martin, who still stood a few feet behind her.

An electric crackle sound shot through the air. Martin stiffened, his body jerking and his eyes wide, then fell to the floor.

Rachel saw him go down, heard the sound, but couldn't react fast enough. Her first impulse was to go to him, but she checked that and instead tried to slam her door closed.

Stephanie threw herself at the office door.

Rachel bucked against the sudden force, digging her heels into the smooth floor, but sliding backward.

Stephanie slithered her slender form through the crack of the door and swung her hand toward Rachel's face.

Rachel turned aside, but not fast enough.

A painful thud to the side of her head shattered her vision into a million stars. And then blackness...

TEN

"Rachel? Rachel?"

Jane's voice jolted Rachel awake, sending a current of pain sizzling through her brain. She screwed her eyes shut, feeling the cold of the linoleum floor and pinpricks of dirt particles against her cheek.

And metal. She smelled metal.

She was smelling her own blood.

"Andrew, come quick," Jane was saying. She must be on her cell phone calling the other security guard.

"Martin?" Rachel whispered. Where was Martin? Was he okay?

"He's fine. He's just still weak."

She tried to raise her head, but the dizziness that attacked her made her stomach heave. No, she didn't want to throw up on her office floor.

The lab doors unlocked and opened, and footsteps hastened close. "Dr. Grant! Martin!" Andrew cried.

"Did you call an ambulance?" Jane asked. "We need to get them to a hospital."

"I can get up," Rachel croaked. She took a

deep breath, then slowly pushed away from the floor, supported by Jane's hands. The ground tilted, but she managed to sit upright, leaning against the open door, which lay flush against her office wall.

Andrew was helping a shaky Martin also get up from the floor.

"Martin, are you all right?" she asked him.

"Dazed," he mumbled. "Shaky. She hit me with a stun gun."

She had suspected as much.

Rachel slowly glanced to the side. Her computer tower was completely gone, only a nest of wires remaining.

Jane followed her gaze. "Don't think about that now."

"It was Stephanie," Rachel whispered.

Martin nodded slowly, his mouth pulled in a regretful grimace. "I let my guard down, Dr. Grant. I'm sorry."

"You couldn't have known." Rachel closed her eyes briefly. "And after she told me about the job offer, I stopped suspecting her. I thought I was being paranoid."

"We'll get you to the hospital and Detective Carter will get to the bottom of this," Andrew said.

"It's too late…" Rachel closed her throat to the sob rising there. "Stephanie has the scar-cream formula. She has all my data."

"Not all your data," Jane hastened to assure her.

"The backup external drive is still there, and it looks fine. I'll take a look after the police go through everything."

"I thought that since the computer was shut down, no one could get the formulation," Rachel moaned. "It didn't even occur to me that they would just take the computer."

"The hack was a distraction," Jane said, her voice taut. "It made you shut down the computer, so she just swiped the tower. No need for her to know how to break into your computer's security system."

"She called me before the hack happened, so I didn't even connect it to her coming to the lab." Plus she hadn't expected Stephanie, rail thin, cute and girly, to take down two-hundred-fifty-pound Martin.

Or herself, for that matter.

"I'm calling your family." Jane punched a number into her cell phone.

"Edward. Call Edward." Rachel wanted him with her. She needed to hear his voice. Everything was falling apart, but just being with him would make her world seem steadier.

And she wanted him with her when she told her father.

When the nurses finally let Edward, Alex and Jane into Rachel's hospital room, Edward had been on the verge of forcing a doctor to let him see her.

As he entered her room, he zeroed in on her face— strained and pale. Trouble lurked in her eyes as she

looked at her father, who sat in his wheelchair near her bed.

Then she turned her head, her eyes brimming with relief as she saw him.

She didn't see her father's hand reaching out toward hers resting on the covers, as if to touch her or hold her. But upon seeing Edward, Alex and Jane, he drew back his hand.

Edward almost regretted their entrance. "How are you feeling?" he asked her.

She surprised him by grabbing his hand and squeezing. Her fingers were cold and he automatically rubbed them in his warm palm.

"I'm fine," she told him.

"She has a concussion," her sister Naomi said darkly from her seat in the corner. "That's not fine."

Becca discreetly laid a hand on Naomi's arm with a flickering glance at Augustus, and Naomi became more subdued.

Augustus didn't witness the exchange. He sat in his chair with a deep frown, but also anxious eyes that glanced at Rachel every few minutes—quick looks that she didn't notice.

"Where's Monica?" Edward asked. He would have expected the youngest Grant daughter, a nurse, to be by her sister's side.

"She's with Devon, consulting with Rachel's doctor," Naomi said.

"Did Jane tell you what happened?" Rachel asked him.

"Jane didn't tell *us* what happened," her father groused.

Jane gave him a cheeky smile. "You weren't stuck out in the waiting room for the past hour, Uncle Aggie."

"I told you everything, Dad," Rachel objected.

"You also had a knock to your head for most of it," Becca retorted. "Go ahead, Jane."

Jane shrugged. "After Rachel told me someone had tried to hack into her computer remotely, I drove to the spa. I found Martin on the floor of the lab, weak and trying to wake Rachel, who was passed out on the floor of her office."

"How is Martin?" asked Rachel.

"Fine," Naomi said. "Blaming himself."

"So he should," Augustus said with some heat. "He's supposed to protect—"

"Augustus," Becca chided. "The girl had one of those zapper things. They're supposed to be able to take down cows, you know."

"Aunt Becca, Martin is not a cow."

"Jane?" Augustus interrupted. "You were saying?"

"I called Andrew, the other security guard, who notified the ambulance and the police."

"Horatio was here a few minutes ago talking to Rachel," Becca said, "but he asked me to mention to you that he'd like to speak to Jane later."

Jane nodded. "I checked your computer, Rach, after the ambulance took you away and the police were

done. Your external backup hard drive is fine and you still have all your data."

"Thank God," Augustus said.

Rachel darted a nervous glance at him.

Edward frowned. How had Augustus taken the news about the stolen formulation?

Rachel seemed to shrink into the white hospital bed. "I had just found out exactly what Steve stole from me," she said softly.

"Who's Steve?" asked Alex.

"Steve Schmidt, Rachel's ex-research assistant, who hacked into her computer about two years ago," said Jane. "Rach, I tried finding him, but no luck."

"Where did he live?" Alex asked.

"San Francisco was his last known address."

Alex pulled at his bottom lip. "I might be able to help," he said slowly.

"Jane." Detective Carter appeared in the doorway. "Oh, and Alex. I need to speak to both of you—Jane, I need your statement, and Alex, I wanted to ask about that case we discussed the other day. Unrelated to this one," he assured them all.

"I'll be back," Jane told Rachel.

"Me, too." Alex followed Jane and the detective out of the room.

"Wait." Augustus rolled his wheelchair after them. "Horatio, I want to know how the investigation is going…."

Rachel watched him exit with pained eyes.

Edward leaned in toward her. "How are you really

doing?" He sent a silent blessing on Becca, who distracted Naomi with some bright chatter.

Rachel's mouth trembled, but she kept her composure. "He was so upset," she whispered.

Edward didn't have to ask who she meant. "He seems worried about you."

Rachel's face was a mix of shame, anger, depression. "When I told him about the computer being stolen, he looked like he wanted to blame me but couldn't."

"Rach, I'm sure he didn't."

"But it is my fault." She swallowed. "Why did I let Stephanie into the lab? If I hadn't let her in…"

"You took the precaution of having Martin with her."

"I just…I should have done things differently. I feel sometimes like I can't do anything right. Like I'm a big failure."

He wanted to shake her. "You're not a failure."

"Dad said…" Then she stopped herself. "I know Dad's not always right. In my head, I *know* that. But when things happen, I…" She closed her eyes for a moment. "I can't stop myself from internalizing it all."

And a strong personality like Augustus Grant would compare Rachel's softer nature to her sisters' more vivacious ones and think Rachel was weak. "You're becoming obsessed with your need to please your father." The words shot out of his mouth before he could think of how to soften them, but he knew

they needed to be said. He needed to get through to Rachel.

Her wide hazel eyes showed that she was startled and a little hurt by his bluntness, but he wanted to help break her out of this cycle. "You said it yourself. Your self-esteem is caught up in whether you fail him or not."

"It's not my self-esteem that—"

"Then why is your father's approval of you so important?"

"It's not."

"How would it make you feel if you knew for certain that your father thought you were incompetent?"

She flinched as if she'd been staked in the heart.

"You care more about what your father thinks of you than you do about how God thinks of you." He knew his words were hard, and he had rarely spoken about faith with her. He had never told her how her faith could be so much more than it was.

In that sense, he had failed her. He should have told her this before.

She turned her eyes away from him. Maybe she was embarrassed that he had brought up the topic.

"Rachel, you're a scientist. You're logical. Can't you see that your fear of failure is illogical and irrational?"

A light flickered in her gaze, then was gone again.

"And that irrational fear drives you. It drives you

at work so that you can try to please your father. But your heavenly Father already loves you."

She met his gaze then, her eyes burning. "You say that," she said slowly. "But I don't feel that. I don't know that *here*." She touched her chest. "It might be true, but, Edward, I don't know it."

He caught her final words as the others started filing back into the hospital room.

"Edward, God has to prove it to me."

ELEVEN

Rachel tossed her Eppendorf pipette on the laboratory counter. What was the use? Her formula was gone. Someone else was using it, developing it, maybe even making it better.

Joy Luck Life spa would come out with a scar-reduction cream, but someone else would come out with it, too, and again, the rumors would say Joy Luck Life had stolen or copied someone else. People would say that if there's smoke, surely there's fire—so Joy Luck Life must be guilty.

The only way to prevent that would be if they came out with the product *tomorrow*. Or next week. And that wasn't going to happen.

She rubbed her temple, trying to dispel the throbbing there. After a couple days in the hospital and over a week of rest, she felt better, but was still occasionally plagued by headaches. She had a feeling they were from stress and not the concussion.

Detective Carter said he had a lead on where Steve Schmidt was, although he didn't tell her more than that. He was still looking for Stephanie and the man

who had later tried to break into the lab and tried to steal the laptop.

So far, no luck.

And really, why was she surprised? Lately, she'd felt as if God had abandoned her. The way everything was working out, it certainly seemed that way.

You care more about what your father thinks of you than you do about how God thinks of you.

How did God think of her? It didn't seem to her as if He loved her very much.

Your heavenly Father already loves you.

It seemed as if love was something she chased and never found. Not her father's love, not God's love.

Not Edward's love.

During those months of working with Edward, she'd gotten to know him. The firm yet compassionate way he interacted with his brother, Alex, and the other people working at his greenhouses contrasted with how her father rigidly demanded quality performance from the spa personnel and his own daughters. Edward was phenomenal with the Malaysian basil—plants very difficult to grow—and yet he was so humble about his abilities, which only made him more attractive to her. When they discussed her work, he made her feel so smart and confident. They had spent so many bright moments laughing together. He had gotten her sense of humor in a way her sisters and father never had.

So she had opened herself up. She had been

unguarded with him in a way she opened up only to her sisters. She had felt free to be herself.

And then a couple of months ago he had withdrawn, as if he hadn't liked what he'd seen. As if she wasn't what he wanted.

He had rejected her for being herself.

Lately he seemed warmer toward her, but she couldn't trust him again, not after he had rejected her. She was afraid to open herself up to him again. And as things progressed, she was starting to think that her viewpoint of who God was differed too much from Edward's faith.

Despite her family's faith, despite the fact she had been baptized when she was a teenager, she wasn't sure if she *wanted* to believe in God anymore.

"God—" she spoke to the empty lab "—do You still care about me? It just doesn't seem that way."

Silence. Really, had she expected Him to answer in a booming voice that shook the building?

"Things have been awful, lately." The accusation echoed off the flat walls. "Why are You letting these things happen?"

Anger started to roll in like a fog. "It doesn't seem like You're there for me anymore."

Really, had she ever felt that God was "there for her"? She had heard the phrase spoken by Aunt Becca and her pastor at church, but had she really felt it herself?

"Edward says You love me. If You love me, prove it."

The challenge made her tremble. Would God strike her down? Or would He prove He was there? Or would He not answer such an impertinent demand at all?

"Prove it." She repeated. "Prove…" She stared down at her empty hands. "Prove You're…my Father."

The anger receded, and there was only emptiness.

Suddenly she heard running footsteps in the hallway outside the lab double doors. Rachel jumped off her high lab stool and whirled to face the doors. What was going on? Should she arm herself? What good would that do? Or maybe it was nothing.…

She heard the sound of fumbling at the card-key lock.

Rachel grabbed her pipette, although its light weight felt useless in her hand.

The locks disengaged, startling her. She tightened her grip on the pipette.

Then Edward burst in, and she almost cried out in relief.

"Rachel, Alex found Steve Schmidt's address."

The narrow San Francisco street wasn't particularly dirty, but something about its eerie emptiness made Edward move closer to Rachel as they picked their way past the battered cars parked on the sidewalk. With parking at a premium in the city, the residents had apparently forfeited a safe walkway. However, the street didn't have much traffic, and walking in the middle of it still gave them ample time to see any cars approaching.

Considering his brother had used his contacts to find this address, Edward hadn't expected the neighborhood to be very upscale. A friend of Alex's who owned homes divided into apartments for rent had known another apartment owner who had been willing to search his records and had found Steve listed as a renter in one of his buildings.

"We should have just waited for Detective Carter to do this," he said.

"I need to do this," she replied mulishly. "I need to look in his face. I hired him. I *trusted* him."

The buildings stretched to the sky, their foundations precariously clinging to the steep hillside. Edward and Rachel leaned forward as they climbed, searching the building numbers.

There. Number 307.

It had a garage door, unlike many of the other houses on the street, but the weather-beaten door was padlocked shut and there was a sporty MINI Cooper parked in front of it, a newer car than most of the others on the street.

"I wonder if that's his," Rachel said. "It's about two years old, and he must have been paid a lot to steal my data."

At that moment, a young blonde woman rattled down the rickety stairs that ran along the side of the narrow three-story house. She paused as she saw them, but beyond a tight nod, she squeezed past, clicking her car keys. The MINI Cooper beeped as the car alarm disarmed, and she climbed inside.

Rachel shrugged. "I guess not."

Edward paused to watch the woman, and noticed that she reached down to adjust the driver's seat and slide it closer to the steering wheel.

Maybe Rachel's initial comment had been right.

He took longer strides to catch up with Rachel as she climbed the stairs. They reached the third-floor landing and knocked on a door with an upside down *C* hanging from the middle of it. Remembering the woman and the car, Edward positioned himself closer to the door and tensed as he waited.

They could hear footsteps inside hastening to the door just before it was flung open. "Claudia, I knew you'd—"

Frozen, a tall young man with dark brown hair stared at Rachel for a full second.

Then he tried to slam the door shut.

However, Edward jammed his foot inside the apartment against the door and threw his entire weight against it. He had anticipation and a good fifty pounds on the research associate, and Steve stumbled back into the apartment.

Edward swung the door open wide, and Rachel followed him inside. "Hi, Steve," she said sweetly.

"D-Dr. Grant." The muscles stood out on his thin neck, and his shoulders moved stiffly as he caught his balance against the sagging, faded plaid couch that stood in the center of the spacious living room.

"Not happy to see me? I don't blame you." Rachel's eyes and voice were strangely impassive as she regarded him.

"Of course I'm happy to see you," he quipped with a sickly smile. "Are you here to hire me back?"

Rachel bent to study the ancient television sitting on old telephone books in front of the couch, with a PlayStation 3 beside it. "I would have thought you'd buy a nicer TV with the money they gave you."

"I don't know what you're talking about, Dr. Grant."

"You probably spent it all on the car." Rachel stood up and turned to face him. "I would have gotten a Miata."

Something—some edge in her voice, in her eyes—belied her calm tone, her neutral face. Steve opened his mouth as if to answer her, but that something made the words freeze on his tongue.

"You probably don't even have an aunt who lives in Sonoma, like you told me." Rachel folded her arms. "But I don't think your credentials were fake. You were a slacker, but you did know what you were doing."

As if she didn't expect an answer, she ambled over to the wide picture window that looked out over the city from the front of the house. "As you can see, Edward is a very large man."

Steve shot him a quick, wild look.

"So, Steve, tell me who hired you to steal my data."

Steve glanced at Edward again, this time for a long minute, searching his eyes, measuring his height and stance. Then Steve shook his head. "I'm not telling you. The other guy was bigger."

Rachel whirled toward him a little too quickly. Then she took a short breath and backed down, resting a hand at her throat. "Who was he?"

Steve shook his head again. "No way." His hands, dangling at his sides, twitched.

One of Steve's pinky fingers looked as if it had been broken.

A thug, maybe, had taken care of the transaction with Steve—hiring him, paying him and leaving a reminder to make sure he wouldn't talk to anyone else.

Like them.

Rachel wandered to the other end of the living room, where the dingy carpet gave way to linoleum and the open kitchen boasted dirty pots tilted in the sink and piled on the electric stove. Next to the kitchen stood a small wooden desk with an old laptop. Rachel touched a key and an old video game popped up on the screen.

"I'm assuming this means you didn't hack into my computer yourself," she said. "I would expect a hacker's desk to look more like my cousin Jane's— full of machinery and better games."

Steve's neck flushed, but he remained silent.

"I guess I was right," Rachel continued. "You were hired to sneak your 'girlfriend,' or the real hacker, into my lab. You hadn't worked for me long enough to realize that the security guard did a lab walk-through every few hours, so he interrupted her. She left a time stamp on my computer."

At this, Steve smirked. "You fired me two years ago, Dr. Grant." Not confessing anything, but pointing out that it took her that long to realize something had been stolen.

Edward's hand flexed.

"Yes, I suppose you're right. I didn't notice it very quickly." Rachel's voice was even more calm, as if she were having this conversation with one of her sisters out in their rose garden on a blissful summer day, not in this dusty apartment that smelled like mice.

She turned to face him, her head tilted to the side. "They tried to kill me, you know."

Steve stopped breathing for a moment, then his thin chest rose and fell rapidly under his cartoon T-shirt.

"They'll be after you next," she told him.

"I don't know what you're talking about." His voice came out strained.

"If it were me, I wouldn't trust in any amount of money to keep someone from talking." Rachel nodded at Edward. "We can protect you."

Steve snorted, although his breath came out shakily. "I don't need protection."

Frustration flashed across Rachel's face for a moment, then was gone. "Please just tell us who hired you to steal my data."

"I didn't steal anything."

"Just the name of who paid you to sneak that girl into the lab. That's all I want."

He shook his head, his thin lips pressed tight.

A sliver of fire then cracked through Rachel's expressionless mask, revealing an inferno raging beneath the surface. Her jaw tightened as her eyes burned into Steve. "It was my data…my work…." Her voice shook.

Edward knew she would regret it if she lost control here, in front of this weasel. He stepped forward and pulled her toward the door. "If you change your mind," he told Steve, "you know where to find us." He steered Rachel out of the apartment, a bit surprised that she didn't resist him.

As they closed the door behind them, the same girl who had left the apartment and gotten into the MINI Cooper paused on her way up the stairs. "Oh," she said, surprised. "Were you visiting Steve?"

"Yes," Edward said, not quite trusting Rachel to answer calmly.

"I'm Claudia. Are you friends of his?"

He shook his head. "I don't know if you want to talk to him right now."

Her eyes widened. "Is he okay? I know he can be a jerk sometimes, but…"

"He's fine," Rachel said, her voice even. She squeezed past the girl, heading down the stairs. "But it may not be in your best interests to be around him for the next few hours."

Alex had promised to give them a couple hours' head start, but by now, he would have told Detective Carter about locating Steve's address.

Steve's next visitors would be the police.

TWELVE

They had gone all that way for nothing.

Rachel picked at her pasta, seeing Steve's smug face instead of the angel hair. For a moment, near the end of the visit, her frustration had been molten magma, bubbling and boiling thickly. She had wanted to launch herself at him, to shake him out of his defiance.

"Rachel."

Edward's voice made her blink, and she saw the hardly touched chicken, tomatoes and basil of her dinner in front of her eyes once more.

"The restaurant's closing," he said. "Let's get you home."

They hadn't spoken much on the drive back to Sonoma. He hadn't even asked her if she was hungry before turning into the restaurant parking lot. Probably because she would have told him she didn't want to eat. He had forced her to order something anyway.

He paid their check and guided her out of the warm restaurant into the frigid night air.

"Horatio's a good detective," Edward said as they walked to his truck. "We can trust him to—"

A rough hand grabbed her arm and pulled her away from Edward even as he was jerked in the other direction. Off balance, she still managed to swing an arm at her attacker, but she only softly clipped a shoulder.

Her frustration at Steve seemed to pour out of her now, firing her fists as she pummeled the man. She connected with an unshaven jaw, a collarbone, an ear.

Fingers bit into her arms and then she was airborne. She slammed into a car with a painful thump—solid steel that jiggled on small wheels. But no alarm went off to alert the restaurant staff.

She had to set off a car alarm.

She was barely on her feet, sagging against the car. Her back ached from the impact, but she rolled to the side, her hands sliding against the windows, trying to find her feet so she could run. But the man's hands pinned her shoulder against the car.

She kicked, but didn't have a good enough foothold and nearly fell, sliding down the side of the car. He pushed at her again, and a headache slammed her between the eyes, clouding her vision for a moment.

When it cleared, she suddenly recognized the man attacking her.

The same one who had tried to get into the card-key doors at the spa. The one Naomi had said tried to steal her laptop.

"You!" She tried to claw at his face, but he shoved a forearm against her neck and pinned her to the car, fumbling for something in his jacket with his other hand.

"Rachel!" Edward wrestled with another man, although she couldn't see clearly. The parking lot was dark and they were too far away from the closest streetlight.

She couldn't let them hurt Edward.

She stamped her foot hard on the man's instep.

"Ooof!"

His arm across her throat loosened, and she jabbed a fist into where she hoped his solar plexus was.

She was free.

She couldn't scream—her throat had closed up. She stumbled toward a sedan parked several yards away. The car alarm. If she could set off the car alarm...

"I'll kill your boyfriend!"

She hesitated, looked over her shoulder.

The other man struggled with Edward. It looked as if they were fighting for control of a gun, but the attacker was a few inches taller and broader across the shoulders. "Shoot her!" the man told Rachel's attacker.

Then she noticed the man she recognized from the spa held a gun pointed right at her.

She wasn't very far away. He had a perfect shot.

And in that moment, everything slowed down. She saw everything in minute detail.

The man's eyes were big and white as they stared

into hers. His mouth pulled wide as he gritted his teeth.

His fingers moved against the handle of the gun.

Oh, God.

And suddenly she understood—the vastness of the universe God had created, the mystery of the life He gave to everything in it, the unknown of death that only God could fathom.

And how small she was. How fleeting her life. How inconsequential she was.

And the immense contrast of how much He loved her despite all that.

Staring down the barrel of that gun, staring into that man's eyes, she had only one thought.

Lord, I surrender.

One heartbeat. Then another.

And still the man waited. Hesitated.

"Shoot her!" the other man shouted again.

But he didn't.

Suddenly Edward swung around, using the centrifugal force of his movement to throw his attacker into the man pointing the gun at her. The two men went down in a heap.

The gun clattered to the asphalt, and there was a cracking sound as it went off. She instinctively flinched and dropped to the ground, expecting a bullet to hit her, but miraculously, nothing happened.

"Hey!" A voice from the restaurant shouted.

She turned and rose to her feet in time to see the

two men running off, and in time for Edward to pull her roughly into his arms.

She was safe.

But for the first time, she became aware of another presence with her.

She felt Him. A sense that she was not alone. That she wouldn't be alone even if Edward weren't there.

He had been there for her. And He was with her still.

She held Edward close until her racing heart had slowed, breathing in his musk and pine, feeling the thud of his own heart.

Then she pulled away slightly. He reluctantly loosened his hold on her.

She reached up, drew his head down and kissed him.

He gasped against her mouth. But then his arms pulled her tighter and he sank into the kiss. It seemed as if he poured into her all his relief and care.

She drew him closer. She wanted him closer. It felt as if this was where he belonged.

He broke off the kiss and pressed his cheek against hers, content to hold her tight against him. "I was afraid," he whispered. "I thought…"

She knew what he thought. She had thought the same thing.

They held each other, feeling the warmth of their embrace and the chill of the night air.

She still felt God's presence with her.

* * *

He had thought he would have to watch her die right in front of him.

Edward remained close to Rachel as the police sergeant explained he would be taking their statement.

"Where's Detective Carter?" Edward asked the young man.

"He'll be here," the sergeant said. "He was out of town for most of today, but he radioed to say he'd be here in a few minutes."

Out of town. Probably in San Francisco, talking to Steve Schmidt. Would Horatio have gotten more out of the research associate than they had? Would he be able to arrest him?

Hopefully the detective wouldn't arrive too quickly. Edward wasn't looking forward to confessing that they had visited Steve before the police did.

Rachel explained what had happened to her, how the man had pulled her away from Edward, how she had fought back, how she'd recognized him as the same man who'd tried to get into the spa lab, how he had pinned her against the car—she pointed to an old Crown Victoria parked nearby, which apparently belonged to one of the restaurant chefs. The police had discovered the dropped gun near the front tire, so they hadn't allowed the chef to drive home.

"I heard Edward cry out," she said. The look she gave him was a strange mixture of worry and relief. "So I stomped on the man's instep and hit him in the gut."

Edward blinked at her. He'd been so busy wrestling with the other man that he hadn't noticed how she'd escaped. A few weeks ago, he wouldn't have thought that sweet, calm Rachel would fight back that way.

"I couldn't scream," she said, and her voice wavered as her eyes unfocused, remembering. "So I ran for the other car to try to trip the alarm. The man said he'd kill Edward, and I turned and saw him pointing a gun at me."

Edward had seen her bolt away, and he had concentrated on getting free. But when his attacker had yelled to the other man, "Shoot her," Edward had hesitated in fear for her.

He'd seen her shocked, frightened, frozen in place. He'd seen the man pointing the gun at her.

And then a look came over her face, a look he couldn't explain. She had closed her eyes once, and when she opened them, it was as if she didn't see the gun, she didn't see the man. She saw something else that made her face relax, that instilled strength in her eyes.

And the man hadn't fired.

"The man hesitated," she told the sergeant. "I don't know why." She finished giving her statement, and then the policeman turned to Edward.

"The man attacked me from behind," he said. "I saw the other one pull Rachel away from me."

"You said he had a gun?"

"I saw it right away in his hand, so I grabbed at it. We were wrestling for a while—after a few minutes, I was losing my grip because my hands were sweating and I couldn't keep hold of his wrists."

Up until that point when he felt his fingers slide over the man's skin, he had felt mostly anger and determination. But when he realized he might not be able to take the gun from him or even hold on to the man's arms, panic had been like a rivulet of ice water running down his back. He had feared for Rachel, for himself.

"I saw Rachel run away from the man, but then my attacker said twice, 'Shoot her.' The second time, I took advantage of my attacker's distraction and shoved him into the one holding the gun."

And he'd prayed the gun wouldn't go off and shoot Rachel. But he hadn't been able to think of what else he could do to stop the man from killing Rachel. He'd been almost crazed with desperation.

"The gun fell and went off, and someone from the restaurant came out. The two men ran off," he finished.

The sergeant's eyes were grave as they turned to Rachel. "Dr. Grant, I know a lot of things have been happening at the spa lately, but I'll ask anyway. Do you know why anyone would want to kill you?"

She closed her eyes, and a pained look crossed her face. "Whoever paid Stephanie to steal the scar-reduction-cream formulation will be developing their own product, but it will still take time to raise the plants and perfect the formula." She swallowed. "If I die, the Joy Luck Life spa can't release our cream. At least, not anytime soon. It clears the way for whoever stole my formula by eliminating their only competition."

In all the excitement and worry of tonight, he hadn't fully realized the whys of the attack. But now the full implications of Stephanie's theft slammed into him.

Rachel's life was now forfeit.

Not on my watch.

He needed to keep her safe until these people could be discovered and arrested, somewhere safer than her home or the spa. Somewhere no one knew about.

Mama's farm.

When the sergeant had finished with his questions, Edward pulled Rachel aside. "We need to move you somewhere safe."

Her eyes were wide and dark in the feeble light from the streetlight. She looked small and helpless. "Our home has an alarm—"

He grasped her by the shoulders. "Your father is the only man in the house, and he's in a wheelchair." He knew it was harsh, but he had to make her see how much danger she was in.

Her eyes faltered and blinked. "The lab…"

"Are you going to sleep there for days? Weeks? Whoever is after you knows that you'll be there, working on the scar cream."

"What else can I do?" she burst out. "Hide in my room? I won't go down without a fight."

The fierceness in her face surprised him, but it also made him want to kiss her again. "Rachel, someone wants you dead. I can't stand by and let that happen."

She paused, and then her hand reached up to cup his cheek, her fingers soft as an orchid petal against his skin.

"I want to move you to my mother's house."

Her brow wrinkled. "Your mother?"

"Mama's farm is deep in Sonoma County. It's hard to find if you don't know where it is, and the lay of the land makes it difficult for anyone to sneak up on the house without being seen."

"Your mother isn't going to want a stranger in her home for possibly weeks."

"She won't mind, especially when she finds out why."

"The spa has two guards at all times."

"Mama's farm would have me and Alex, and also my farm manager and eight ranch hands during the day, and three of them who stay in the house at night."

Rachel blinked. "So many in your mother's house?"

"They're Alex's friends from prison. I gave them jobs working Mama's farm."

She gave him a half smile.

"No one connected with the spa would know about Mama's farm."

She laid a hand on his chest. "Edward—"

He folded her hand in his own and held it close

to him. "I want to move you out there as soon as possible."

"Let me think about this first," she pleaded. "And I need to talk to my father." A shadow passed over her eyes, but he couldn't be sure in the darkness.

"What do you think you were doing?" roared a familiar voice.

Detective Carter threw himself out of a police car before it had even come to a complete stop in the restaurant parking lot. He stormed toward them. "I want to know what you thought you were doing. I expected better from you, Edward," the detective raged.

"I told Alex to talk to you after he'd told us about Steve's address."

"He should have come to me first," Horatio ground out. "You had no business talking to him before I did."

"You don't understand. I needed to talk to him," Rachel said. "I needed to see his face. I needed to look into his eyes. I was the one who hired him. I was the one who fired him when I thought he was just a disrespectful research assistant." Her breath came in gasps now. "I had to stare into his face when I asked him why he did it."

Horatio had calmed during her tirade, but the lines around his mouth were still deep and grim. "Dr. Grant, you are not a police officer."

"I was his boss and his *victim*." She pressed her lips together.

Edward put an arm around her and addressed the detective. "Did you arrest him?"

"We didn't find him." Horatio's eyes were hard as they fell on Edward. "His girlfriend told us he had taken off and she didn't know where. She also gave us a nice description of the two of you." He frowned at both Edward and Rachel.

"He's gone?" she whispered.

"You should have left it to me," Horatio growled as he turned away. "Because of your visit to him, we might never find Steve Schmidt."

THIRTEEN

For breakfast, Rachel's father had coffee, eggs and the news that his oldest daughter's life was in jeopardy.

"Why didn't you tell me this last night?" he demanded, his fist pounding on the wheelchair armrest.

"You were already asleep," Rachel said.

"And I wasn't about to let her wake you," Monica added, with a supporting nod in Rachel's direction.

The gesture made Rachel realize for the first time that her sisters tended to defend her to her father when they could. On one hand, she felt vindicated, but on the other, she wondered if it only hurt her cause with her father because she never stood up for herself.

She remembered the rose garden.

Her shoulder blades stiffened. "What would you have been able to do if I told you last night, Dad? We already reported the incident to the police."

Monica's eyebrows rose slightly as she regarded her sister, but she didn't say anything.

Her father frowned at her. "I had a right to know. This is still my roof you're living under."

"You'd only have lost sleep if I told you last night," Rachel replied.

"I, not you, determine what I lose sleep over," he said rather petulantly.

He was being exacerbating, but Rachel became aware that perhaps his grouchiness stemmed from concern for her.

Then he dispelled that warm thought with his next words. "You should have been taking more precautions. You knew they'd gotten the formula."

Naomi gasped.

"Dad!" Monica barked.

"Augustus!" Aunt Becca sputtered in her tea.

Rachel slammed her hand down on the breakfast table. "I have spent two weeks being escorted everywhere, Dad. You can't say I haven't tried to stay safe."

The silence was awful. Her father's eyes burned into her, but Rachel didn't back down. She wouldn't let her sisters defend her this time. She wouldn't let her father accuse her of what wasn't her fault—not this time.

Not ever again.

Aunt Becca cleared her throat. "At least you're all right, dear."

Her words prompted Monica to get up from the table and start collecting her father's medicines to dispense, although Rachel noticed a prescription bottle that Monica didn't normally open when she gave Dad his meds.

"You should stay at the spa," her father said.

Rachel sipped her tea, curling her numb fingers around the cup to warm them. "Edward suggested I hide out at his mother's farm."

"No."

She flinched at his response, an automatic reaction, but then she sat up straight in her chair. She wouldn't be cowed again. "Why not?" Not that she had made a decision about it yet.

"I don't know what your boyfriend, Horatio, is doing," he said to Aunt Becca. "Why hasn't he caught those who are behind this?"

"He's doing the best he can," Becca shot back. "These people have been working on this for two years and they don't want to be found."

"What does that have to do with my not staying at Edward's mother's house?" Rachel asked.

"If the police can't find these people, we have to beat them at their own game," Dad said. "Put out the scar-reduction cream early. They can't produce their own product for a while, even if they do have the formula."

Even though she had considered this option to pursue, her father's vocalizing it made something ignite in her chest. She shot to her feet. "What, do you expect me to stay day and night at the spa until the product is finished?"

"No, but—"

"Dad, I just lost my research associate."

"A traitor whom you hired," he fired back.

"That's unfair, Dad," Naomi objected, but Rachel put up her hand to quiet her.

This was her battle. "That doesn't help the situation, Dad."

"We need to do something. I won't stand for these people sabotaging my business."

"Your business?" Aunt Becca set her teacup down with a snap. "What about your daught—"

"Thanks, Dad." Rachel stood up straight and glared down at him. Something inside of her had severed. "I now know that this product is more important to you than me."

Her bitter words echoed off the walls. A part of her just wanted to curl up under the table and cry. The other part wanted him to justify himself, to explain why he was being like this. And not because her sisters jumped into the fray to defend her, but because he respected *her,* Rachel, enough to be held accountable for his words.

He'd gone white. Rachel's vision had narrowed to just his faded green eyes, the whites of his eyes, his papery skin.

"Well, Dad?" she demanded. She would have an answer. Something inside of her had changed. Something from last night had changed her. Somehow, he didn't frighten her as he used to.

His eyes dropped from hers, and his face seemed to sag. "That's not true," he whispered.

"That's how I feel, Dad. Every time you rant about

what I should have done to prevent all this from happening. Do you really believe it's all my fault?"

"No...no...." His voice had become fragile. "I just wanted to push you to be your best."

"I am my best, Dad, and it's not enough for you."

"That's not true."

"You don't push Naomi or Monica this way." Time to go all out, to say everything she had been feeling but hadn't ever said. "You don't demand from them the things you demand from me."

"Now you're exaggerating," he said, his voice gaining some of its forcefulness back.

"No, I'm not."

"No, she's not," Aunt Becca said.

Dad stared at his sister-in-law. "What?"

"Naomi disagrees with you all the time. Monica argues with you loud enough to bring down the roof. But Rachel always agrees with you." As she spoke to Dad, Aunt Becca's eyes grew harder than Rachel had ever seen them before. "And because she does, you don't respect her. Or her work for you."

"I do respect her," he protested weakly.

"You don't understand me," Rachel said firmly.

He closed his eyes, and a spasm of pain crossed his face. "Your mother did."

His words seemed to make everything stop—the crisp breeze from the open window, her heartbeat, her breathing. Then she blinked, and everything restarted.

"You have to understand." His voice wavered and

he looked at her with desperate eyes. "I need to *do* something." He grasped his wheelchair with clawed hands and shook it, once. "You are my daughter, and I need to *do* something."

Because in that chair, he was more helpless than he had ever been in his life, Rachel realized.

His face fell. "I'm sorry," he whispered. "I was pushing you because I was just trying to do something."

Rachel jumped at the feel of a hand on her shoulder.

Monica squeezed lightly, then released her. At the same time, she handed some pills to Dad. "Here, Dad. Take your meds."

"I saw you add a dose of that sedative," he grumbled, but he took them all.

"It'll start working fast, so let's get you to your room." Monica took the back of his wheelchair and turned him around.

But he reached out toward Rachel, who grasped his strong, bony hand. He didn't say anything, but he held her for a moment, then let her go as Monica pushed him out of the kitchen.

Naomi draped her arm around Rachel, while Aunt Becca pulled her close with an arm around her waist. They stood there for a few seconds, and Rachel tried to decide if she wanted to cry or not.

"I'm proud of you, Rach." Naomi kissed her cheek, then let go.

Suddenly, the doorbell sounded once, twice,

three times in rapid succession, punctuated by a fist pounding the front door.

At first, Rachel resented the intrusion, but as the knocking continued in urgency, tension began to coil in her stomach.

"Gracious." Aunt Becca hurried out of the kitchen into the entrance foyer, followed by Rachel and Naomi. She yanked open the door.

Edward almost fell into the foyer, catching himself on the door frame. His eyes found Rachel. "Pack up your stuff."

She started to shake her head. "I haven't decid—"

"No time." He strode into the house. "I'm taking you to Mama's farm today. Right now."

"Edward—"

"Detective Carter is on his way," Alex said, following his brother into the house. "I happened to be with him when he got the news."

"About what?"

"Steve Schmidt is dead."

Edward's mother, Carmella, had a smile like a full-blown Spanish rose. "For the hundredth time, I don't mind you staying with me." She handed Rachel a plate with a sandwich and pushed her down onto a sofa cushy enough to drown her. "Most of the time, my boys spend more time working than with their mama."

Edward rolled his eyes in a boyish gesture Rachel

had never seen him use before as he flung himself into a recliner opposite the sofa. "Mama, you only like talking about celebrity gossip."

"Yeah, Mama." Alex entered the living room with an overstuffed sandwich in his hands. "If you talked about cars—"

"Or orchids," Edward said.

"—we'd spend hours talking with you." Alex kissed his mother's cheek good-naturedly before sitting down in another recliner and taking a gigantic bite from the sandwich.

Their bantering eased the tightness in Rachel's shoulders, the lingering effects of the news about Steve Schmidt.

They hadn't actually come straight here to Carmella's house this morning. Detective Carter had questioned Edward and her exhaustively when he arrived at Rachel's home, and then she'd insisted on being taken to the lab first to get some papers and fill a flash drive with some clinical-data numbers she needed to crunch.

"What do you expect me to do at your mother's house?" she reasoned with Edward when he protested. "Work in the fields? Clean the bathrooms?"

She actually had no objection at being put to work, even if it was just weeding the fields, but she also knew it would be dangerous for her to be out in the open. Alex had told her that she could use his computer at his mother's home, so when she arrived, after greeting Carmella, she had gone to the second-floor office to boot up the computer and insert the flash drive before heading downstairs again at Carmella's insistence on feeding her.

Edward's cell phone interrupted them. He glanced at the caller ID before giving his mother a rueful smile and leaving the living room to take the call.

Carmella sighed. "So busy, that boy. I don't think he realizes how much like his father he is."

"No, Mama, he's nothing like Papa." Alex's tone was still jovial, but his face had stilled to a more serious cast.

"But he's always working."

Rachel looked at the doorway Edward had passed through, although she couldn't see him. Carmella's words surprised her. They seemed to imply Edward's father had worked too hard.

"Mama, you're exaggerating." Alex finished the last bite of his sandwich. "Edward keeps strict work hours and if he can't finish something by quitting time, he puts it off to tomorrow. And he doesn't work overtime unless it's scheduled."

Rachel remembered being frustrated when he insisted on postponing something for her basil plants until the next day. A hazy picture of Edward's family life—perhaps before his father died—began to form in her mind.

"You're right," Carmella said with a sigh. "I know he puts his family first."

Unspoken was the thought, *Unlike his father.*

Rachel's curiosity must have shown on her face,

because Carmella said, "Edward and Alex's father was a bit of a workaholic."

"Don't soften it," Alex told her in a quiet voice, "or Rachel will think Edward's reaction to him is too extreme."

Carmella's face pinched tight for a moment as she remembered something. "He didn't know how to be a better father," she said weakly.

"He could have been a better man," her son retorted. "He could have at least been there for you, if not for us."

"He had passion…"

"For money. Not for his work."

"No, he loved his work."

"He was obsessed with his work because it made him money."

Alex's words thrummed a sour chord in Rachel's heart. Some could say she had become obsessed with her work, too, although not for the money. Was his father's neglect the motivation behind Edward's coolness toward her sometimes when she harped about the things she needed to get done at the lab?

Alex's tone and attitude told Rachel this was an argument they'd had many times before. "Mama, I know you don't want to speak ill of the dead, but Papa's actions spoke what he never said. He failed us. He neglected you."

"Alex," Carmella protested. "Now you're exaggerating."

"What else would you call it when he didn't attend

Edward's college graduation, or the opening day of his greenhouse business?"

Rachel swallowed her gasp. No matter how vehemently her father argued with her sister Monica, he'd been so proud to see her get her nursing degree. He'd been equally as proud when Rachel got her Doctorate in Dermatology, and he'd thrown a party on Naomi's first official day working for him as a massage therapist.

"You were the one raising us, Mama."

"He provided for all of us," Carmella said. "It wasn't as if I was a single parent struggling with a single income."

"We could tell it hurt you, Mama."

Carmella cast an embarrassed glance at Rachel. "Maybe we shouldn't talk about this…."

Rachel didn't realize until that moment that she had leaned forward in her seat. She was anxious to hear all these things she had never been told even though she'd known Edward and Alex through their years in high school.

She couldn't quite interpret Alex's look in her direction, but he said, "I think Rachel needs to know about Dad, and about how it impacted Edward."

Carmella grasped at the topical tangent. "Edward is a good boy," she said, taking Rachel's hand. "But I'm sure you know that by now."

"Edward has his priorities straight," Alex said.

"Yes, Edward would never…" Carmella broke off, embarrassed.

"Edward would never treat his own family the way our father treated us," Alex finished frankly.

The way I treat him.

A chasm had opened in her stomach. This was why he'd withdrawn from her a few months ago, around the same time she'd ramped up her work hours on the scar-reduction cream.

He would never become involved with a woman who had the same priorities as his father, so he had stepped back, made their relationship purely professional again.

She had felt so rejected. They had been getting along so well. She had been free to be herself with him, and when he withdrew, she thought it was because he hadn't liked the real Rachel.

Well, he had seen the real Rachel—the one who spent hours at the lab, trying to please her father.

If his father's obsession had been money and success, then hers had been her dad's approval. And they both had pursued their obsessions to the point of shoving aside the other people in their lives.

Carmella was looking at her with concern, so Rachel tried to wipe her emotions from her face. She gave a brief smile.

"I'm sorry," Carmella said. "I shouldn't have mentioned all this."

"No, don't…"

Carmella shook her head. "I talk too much. I air too much laundry—"

"No…."

"Rachel, let me show you Edward's arbor." Alex rose to his feet with a gentle look at his mother and an understanding one at Rachel. "He built it last year for Mama."

Rachel bundled up in her bulky winter coat because the air seemed frostier here out in the heart of the Russian River Valley than near the city of Sonoma. Alex led her through the back door. The outside floodlights sprang to life as they stepped off the back porch, and they walked toward a trellised bench in the backyard.

Rachel sank onto the chilled seat, but it began to warm to her body heat. In her thick coat, she was comfortably cozy, with the cold air pinching her cheeks.

"Look up," Alex said.

She did, and the air expanded in her lungs. The entire Milky Way spread across the sky in a swath of glittering diamonds. The sky looked huge, bigger than she'd ever seen it before.

"Close to Sonoma, the lights from the city and the vineyards hide the stars," Alex said. "I like coming to Mama's farm because it's far away from any clutter."

"I've lived in Sonoma all my life," Rachel breathed, "and I've never seen anything like it." She felt small and yet she was a part of that expansive sky.

"It reminds me of how big God is," Alex said. "But at the same time, I feel loved."

She drank in the beauty of those stars, that midnight

sky. This was the God who had been with her when that man pointed the gun at her. This was the God whose touch to her that night had changed something inside her.

But was it a good change? She remembered her father's shocked face this morning...and the tight clasp of his hand on hers.

"I'm sorry about your father," she said. "But I'm sure he loved you. Maybe he just didn't know how to say it." Like her father.

But Alex shook his head. "I don't know, to be honest. After I got out of prison, I went to Papa and told him how I'd become a Christian. But he refused to speak to me because my arrest shamed him."

"He wouldn't even speak to you?"

"He never spoke to me up to the day he died."

She couldn't imagine that. Even her father would get over himself and speak to her, no matter how upset he got. Her heart ached for Alex. "How can you stand it?" she whispered.

He surprised her with a smile that shone brighter than the stars above them. "I already had the love of my heavenly Father. I have His love and approval, and I didn't need my earthly father's approval."

Rachel was dumbfounded.

"That's not to say it didn't hurt," he said, his face sobering. "And I was angry for a while. But I've learned to stand secure in my confidence in Christ's love. He won't turn away from me the way Papa did. Ever." He smiled then at the sky above. "I have peace."

And he did. There was that something in his face that showed a sort of emotional freedom, despite the neglect and then rejection from his father.

It came from God. And God had given it to her, too.

"I've been lying to myself," she said.

"How?"

"It hasn't just been Dad pushing me in my work. I've been perpetuating the lie that he only loved me when I succeeded. I wanted his approval over all else."

"You already have God's approval," Alex said. "When you believed in His son, Jesus Christ."

All those years of being a Christian, but never realizing how much she was loved. By God, and by her father.

"God has always loved you," Alex said, as if reading her mind. "And He isn't like your father. Like my father."

No, He wasn't. She could now see Him in a new light.

She would still struggle with her priorities. She would still struggle against habit and trying to please her father. But she now knew, deep inside her, that she had been freed from bondage. From a lie.

"Over here, Edward," Alex called out.

Edward's broad shoulders were silhouetted against

the outside floodlights as he strode toward them. "Mama's frantic. The coffeemaker is broken."

"Again? I told her to get a new one." Alex rose. "Here, I warmed the seat for you." He headed into the house.

Edward and Rachel sat in silence for a while, a silence both awkward and comfortable. The knowledge she'd just gained about his father, the realization about God and her own father, the beauty of God's creation above her and the protectiveness of the man beside her—they bubbled up into words that spilled out of her.

"Edward, this is the best night of my life."

FOURTEEN

For a moment Edward wondered if she had a fever. "Drinking Mama's bad coffee, eating turkey sandwiches, shivering out here in the backyard?"

She laughed on a light breath, a frosty cloud wafting in her face. "I suppose that statement did seem to come out of nowhere." Her features stilled, and she turned serious eyes to him. "Something happened to me last night," she said, "when I stared down the barrel of that gun."

His grip on her hand tightened. He'd never felt so helpless as he had at that moment, watching that man point that gun at her and being held back in his struggles with the other attacker.

"You know how they say your life flashes before your eyes? Mine didn't, exactly." She looked up at the bright sky. "But I suddenly felt like I wasn't alone."

"You're never alone. God is always with you." The words were automatic, words he'd read in his Bible and heard at church, but as he said them he knew that he believed them and that they applied directly to her.

"I don't think I've ever really believed that before yesterday," she said. "Isn't that sad? I've been a Christian for most of my life."

"You never liked talking about your faith with me," he said.

"I know. It made me uncomfortable. I didn't really know God. But then at that moment, all I could think was, 'Lord, I surrender.' And then everything was suddenly okay."

He remembered the strange peace that had settled on her face when she closed her eyes.

"Alex told me about how your father treated him after prison."

His jaw flexed involuntarily. Despite what his father had done to him, he hated even more what he'd done to Alex.

"But Alex has such a deep peace in him," she said. "He made me see that my heavenly Father loves me like no one else can. I don't need to please my dad because God already thinks the world of me." She laughed, a sound more freeing than any he'd heard from her in the past few months. "It's as if my self-esteem got a booster shot."

He'd been aware of something different in her, but now he could clearly see it. She had transformed.

God inside her had transformed her.

He should have been trusting God more. He had only been trusting in what he could see with his eyes—Rachel's drive, the circumstances around her. He hadn't been trusting in God—or, even worse, he hadn't been praying for her—to see how much deeper her faith could be, to see how her determination to succeed had been motivated by a desire to please her father. He hadn't trusted, but God had been working in her anyway.

No thanks to his own witness to her.

He reached over to hold her hand in both of his own, and the heat warmed his chilled fingertips. He'd been slowly seeing, in the past few weeks, that her workaholic tendencies were different from his father's. But when he saw her intensity for her lab work, he'd only reacted out of fear rather than what his heart had been telling him about her.

He touched her face, finding her cheek in the darkness. And then he kissed her.

Her lips were cold, so he warmed them. And he tried to convey all he was sorry for. He understood her now. He would protect her from this unseen enemy.

A familiar soft click echoed across the yard. The floodlights coming on. Nothing to be alarmed about.

Except that the floodlights were already on.

He looked up. The perimeter lights had activated.

Movement in the far corner of the field, just on the edge of the light-sensor range.

He bolted to his feet. "Get in the house," he said. "Alex!"

His brother was already pelting down the back porch, two shotguns in his hands. He tossed one to

Edward, as he was followed by two of the farmhands who stayed at the house, also armed with shotguns.

Alex grabbed Rachel's arm and propelled her into the house. "Lock the door behind you," he told her, then turned back toward Edward. "Julio is upstairs with Mama. They'll protect Rachel, too."

The four of them raced toward where he'd seen the movement. "They didn't know the sensors reached that far," Alex observed as they ran.

Edward motioned with his arm, and they fanned out in different directions, arcing around a lone stand of apricot trees. There was nowhere else an intruder could hide because of the flatness of the land.

Edward cocked the shotgun. He'd only loaded the guns with rock salt, but just the sound was menacing. He hoped it would scare the intruder into giving up or bolting.

The man bolted.

There were two of them. One surprised Alex and shoved him to the ground.

The other raced across the field toward the country road at the back of the property. Edward took aim and fired, but he knew the man was already too far away. One of the two farmhands, who was on the far side of the stand of trees, raced after him, while the second headed toward Alex.

The other intruder stumbled after his partner, but he twisted around to aim a handgun at Alex and he fired.

"Alex!" Abandoning his pursuit, Edward slid to the ground next to his brother.

There was a dark blotch on Alex's shirtsleeve.

"I'm fine," Alex said through gritted teeth. "The bullet winged me."

Edward ripped open the sleeve and sopped up the blood around the wound. Alex grunted.

He was right. There was a bloody score across his upper arm, but it wasn't deep. "You might need stitches."

"I've had worse injuries, working on the farm."

It was true. As boys, they'd been crazy to play as they had around the large farm equipment, and even as men working the farm, Alex still had a slightly reckless streak.

The two farmhands came back, breathing heavily. "They got away in a car parked on that access road."

"Thanks, guys," Edward said.

The two men nodded, then headed toward the house.

"Help me up," Alex said, and Edward pulled him to his feet.

"Mama's going to fuss," Edward warned him.

Alex grinned. "She'll give me an extra slice of her chocolate cake." Then he sobered. "What about Rachel?"

Edward sighed, looking back at the farmhouse, lit up with the porch lights and the outside floodlights. "She isn't safe here. I thought she would be."

"Not your fault." Alex headed toward the house slowly, on shaky feet.

Edward resisted helping him.

"You tried to make sure you weren't followed," Alex commented.

"How about Uncle Albert? Think he can help us?" Edward asked.

Albert wasn't really their uncle, but a private investigator friend of Alex's. Not a bad idea. "I'll see him tomorrow," Alex stated.

"No. I'll go. You'll get that looked at." Edward gestured toward Alex's arm. "And then you'll stay here. Protect Rachel."

Alex nodded. "With my life."

Edward hoped it wouldn't come to that.

Rachel hadn't had time alone to talk with Edward since last night, and she wasn't sure if she wanted to talk to him or wanted to avoid him.

She had kissed him in the parking lot. Last night he had kissed her under the stars.

She dwelled on the memory for a sweet moment before reluctantly pushing it aside. The first kiss had been relief she was alive. The second had been moved by the romantic setting. She shouldn't read too much into them both. And in the cold light of day, the danger to her took precedence.

Rachel flipped through a few screens on her computer, worried because she had forgotten to take off the data she'd been working on from Alex's computer.

After Alex had been shot, Edward had whisked her and his mother away to the Grants' home, since the men after her now obviously knew she was at the farm. She had been so frightened, so worried for Alex and Edward, that she hadn't remembered the flash drive. She had a copy of the data here at the spa, but she didn't like leaving it at the farm, where it could be stolen.

She started a statistics program to filter through the results. It would take several minutes, so she got up and exited the card-key secured area to peek into Naomi's office.

Aunt Becca sat opposite Naomi's desk, just clicking off her cell phone. "Oh, good. I was just about to call you. That was Horatio."

"Did the police find anything when they went out to the Villas' farm?"

"They only just finished."

Rachel glanced at Naomi's wall clock. "So late? It's already noon."

"After leaving our house last night, they apparently got lost trying to find the farm and only started collecting evidence early this morning."

"Rach, I don't know how those men found you if even the local police got lost in the dark," Naomi said.

Rachel had wondered the same thing. "I thought of that. I checked my purse, my shoes, my clothes, everything, but I don't think I've been bugged. Not that I know what I was looking for. I'll have Alex look through my clothes when he's feeling better."

"Horatio asked if Alex was okay," Aunt Becca said, "but I told him I haven't seen Alex since he and Monica left for the emergency room last night, after he spoke to you all."

"Alex needed stitches, like Monica said he would," Rachel replied. "Alex called me earlier from the hospital. He was meeting Edward at their uncle Albert's office in San Francisco."

"Edward should have taken you with him rather than leaving you here at the spa," Naomi said. "He must be exhausted after staying up all night guarding our house, and now to drive to the city? You could have shared some of the driving time, at least."

Rachel privately agreed, but Edward had been adamant about leaving her under the protection of the security guards, the outside surveillance video and the card-key locks of the spa...except she'd left her office just now. She glanced guiltily out Naomi's office door at the empty hallway.

Naomi's phone rang. "Hello...? Oh, hi, Edward."

Rachel perked up. "Where is he?"

"Okay, I'll tell her." Naomi hung up. "He's on his way here—he's only a few minutes out. He asks for you to be ready to leave."

"Why didn't he call me?"

Naomi glanced at Rachel's empty lab-coat pocket. "Got your cell phone?"

Her neck set on fire. "Oh. Well, did he say where we're going?"

Naomi shrugged. "He didn't say, but if you don't grill him when he gets here, I sure will."

"Now, he's only concerned for Rachel's safety," Aunt Becca said.

Rachel pounced on Edward when he arrived at the spa a few minutes later. "What's going on?" she asked, before even saying hello.

"Hello to you, too," he said with a raised eyebrows and a half smile, but then he sobered. "Uncle Albert is going to help us find somewhere for you to hole up for a while, at least until the police can find these men."

"Hole up? Like a safe house?" She had visions of a hotel room, nothing to do to keep her worrying mind occupied, and the four walls closing in on her.

He shrugged. "Not sure. Uncle Albert is going to meet us at your house."

"Where's Alex? Wasn't he with you?"

"He drove to your house to pick up Mama and take her home," Edward said. "She called us—she enjoyed chatting with Augustus all day, but she wants to go to her own house now."

"Is that wise?" Aunt Becca asked.

Edward sighed. "No. But it's Mama. We don't really have a choice. She threatened to drive back out there by herself if we don't take her home. I've asked a few more farmhands to stay with her at the house for some extra protection."

"Do you think she's in danger, too?" Naomi asked.

"I hope not, but better safe than sorry. Alex will stay at the house with her." He caught Rachel's eyes with his own. "I'll stay with you."

She wanted to reach out and grab his hand, to convey how much that meant to her. "When is your uncle meeting us?"

"He said he has a few things to take care of first, so a couple hours."

"I hate to ask you this, but I forgot some things at your mother's house."

"Can you leave it there?"

"I don't know if it's that important, but I forgot a flash drive of clinical-trial data on Alex's computer." She gave him an apologetic look. "I was so panicked last night as we were leaving that I forgot about it."

"Did you leave any clothes there?" Naomi asked. "Remember, you were going to ask Alex?"

"That's right." She turned to Edward. "We're not sure how they found out that I was at your mother's farm. I checked my clothes for tracking devices, but would your brother take a look at my things? I'll pick up fresh clothes at home."

"That's a good idea." Edward's cell phone rang, and he glanced at the caller ID before answering. "Hi, Alex."

"Knock, knock," her cousin Jane said from the doorway. "Hey, there's a party in here."

"Oh, I almost forgot you were coming, Jane."

Naomi fumbled with her keys and unlocked her desk drawer. "Thanks for agreeing to look at my laptop today."

"Hey, Rach, how are you doing?" Jane touched her hand. "Uncle Aggie told me about last night when I stopped by the house this morning."

Rachel chatted with Jane until Edward clicked his cell phone shut. "Alex said he's at your house, but Mama's not quite ready to leave," Edward said with a long-suffering look.

Rachel bit back a smile. "He called just to tell you that?"

His expression tensed. "He also said to be careful when we go to Mama's house because the farmhands are all out working the south field today. There's no one at the house."

"Oh, dear," Aunt Becca said. "Maybe you two should go home and have Alex and your mother drive to the farm with you."

"We'll only be at the house a few minutes, and no one knows we're heading there." Edward pulled out his truck keys. "But just to be safe, I'll call Julio and Chase and ask them to meet us at the house."

The first part of the drive was taken up with Edward calling two of his farmhands, friends of Alex's from prison, to ask them to meet them by the time they got there. Then he fielded a few calls from someone at the greenhouses—apparently a handful of his clients had tried to get hold of him but couldn't.

"I'm sorry to be taking you away from your work," Rachel said as he hung up.

"You're more important, Rach." His look toward her reminded her of the molten center of a chocolate lava cake, and she couldn't help smiling. Then he turned his concentration on the winding dirt roads to the farm.

Edward drew the truck right up next to the front porch.

"I'll only be a second." Rachel unbuckled her seat belt. "I know exactly where the flash drive is." She would hate if that data landed in the hands of whoever had stolen her formulation. It wouldn't necessarily help their product development, but it would affirm the results of her formulation and perhaps increase their production schedule.

"Julio, Chase," Edward called as he exited the truck and headed into the house.

Rachel's cell phone rang. She dug it out of her purse, but she fumbled it in her hand and it started to fall. She bent to snatch it before it hit the ground.

The car window shattered next to her ear.

FIFTEEN

Edward heard the crack of the gun first, then saw the glass from the passenger-side window raining over Rachel's crouched form.

"Rachel!" He bounded down from the front porch and shielded her with his body.

Another shot whistled past his ear to land *thwack!* in his truck door.

"Run!" He pulled her around the front bumper.

"Where's it coming from?" she cried.

There were few trees, no place for a sniper to hide. He peered quickly over the hood of the truck and saw movement near the compost piles several yards away. Another bullet dinged the truck, inches from his head.

Too close for comfort.

He fumbled for his keys. Could he get them both inside the truck without being shot?

More shots hit the vehicle, and the angles changed with each bullet fired.

Whoever shot at them was moving closer.

He grabbed for the door handle.

A series of bullets hit the two outside tires. Edward felt the truck jolt, then start to sag.

Getting away in the truck was out.

He grabbed Rachel's hand and bolted for the corner of the house. Bullets ricocheted off the paneling, sending fragments flying through the air.

The shotguns were inside the house. He needed to get the shotguns.

They raced toward the back door.

Then it occurred to Edward—with all these shots being fired, where were Julio and Chase? They had said they'd meet them at the house.

He jumped up the back porch steps, ready to kick the door in—except it was already wide open, with only the screen door closed over the entrance.

He twisted midstep and ducked, pushing Rachel's head down as a second shooter in the house fired at them through the rear screen door.

"Go!" he shouted, and shoved her in the direction of the vineyard in the north field.

As they ran away from the house, a ringing filtered through his frantic thoughts. Rachel's cell phone ringing again. It sounded faint, as if from the front of the house, maybe near the truck.

"I've got to get my phone!"

"Too late." He pushed her ahead of him even as he reached in his back pocket for his own cell phone.

Bullets flew over their heads, but the vineyard wasn't far away from the house. They dived to the ground between the rows of grapevines, still clothed with withering brown and gold leaves, but full enough to provide some visual cover. Shots fired, and leaves exploded around them as they crawled.

"This way," he whispered, and slithered between grapevine plants to cut across the rows. Rachel followed.

The shots petered off. Edward peered through a mass of vines and leaves and saw two men—the same men who had attacked them at the restaurant—headed across the field toward them, guns raised, but obviously unsure where they were among the mass of grapevines.

"Stay low," he told her.

"We can't stay here," she whispered.

They were trapped. They could crawl through the vineyard for only so long before they were caught. The land was too flat for them to make a run for it.

He dialed Alex on his cell phone. It rang once.

Twice.

Three times.

A bullet shattered a woody grapevine a few rows away. Then another.

Trying to flush them out?

His call to Alex went to voice mail.

He had to try calling the other farmhands. But how long would it take them to get here? They were all the way on the other side of the property in the south field.

Would it be too late by the time they got here? Would they arrive just to be gunned down?

He started to dial on his cell phone, but a bullet pinged a grapevine right over their heads, raining leaves and splinters around him. No time to call now—he shoved his cell phone back in his pocket. First he had to get Rachel someplace safer than this vineyard before they were shot. But where?

He tried to visualize the layout of the farm, but his panicked brain couldn't recall more than the vineyard.

He had to calm down. He was in fight-or-flight mode. His logical processing had shut down. The layout of the farm would come to him if he just calmed down.

Lord, please help us.

Then he had a fleeting thought—the ditch.

It ran along the back of the north field, originally for irrigation. Later, his father had tried raising cows for a brief stint and had used it as a natural barrier to keep the animals from wandering too far afield.

Since then, it had become more shallow from erosion and filled with weeds—perfectly hidden from view at ground level unless a person knew it was there or walked within a couple feet of it.

"Come on." He tugged at Rachel's hand to get her to follow him through the grapevines.

They crawled between the largest vines, which were still thick with dying foliage to shield them and also had enough space between the stalks to allow them to slide through without knocking a plant and alerting the men of their position. The shots fired at the plants moved away from them as the men traveled in the opposite direction they were headed. *Thank You, God.* The ditch bordered an empty field with no cover, so the men must have assumed they wouldn't head in that direction, where they would be easily seen.

And shot.

No. He had to focus on keeping them alive for a few minutes longer.

"Stop!" Rachel hissed, grabbing at his ankle.

He twisted around to look at her. Eyes wide, she pointed to a patch of weeds to their left. "I saw something move. Aren't there snakes in vineyards?"

At the word *snake,* his back knotted, but then he remembered the time of year. He squinted around him, felt the nip of the air on his skin despite the warm sunlight, and shook his head. "Too cold for snakes. They're hibernating."

"Are you sure?"

As she spoke, the patch of weeds *did* rustle. He froze.

He'd seen rattlesnakes in this vineyard. But usually in spring or summer, not in October. No rattle meant if it was a rattlesnake, it hadn't yet been alarmed enough to make a sound.

"Don't move," he whispered to her.

But the sound of the two men in the other corner of the vineyard might scare the snake into panicking, especially if they came any closer.

"Back away slowly," he said, sliding along the dirt.

She followed…and then a mouse darted out of the weeds and ran across her foot.

"Eep!" It escaped her lips even as she clapped a hand over her mouth to muffle the sound.

They both froze.

The two men stopped shooting.

Edward counted his heartbeats, thundering in his ears, fast and hard. He moved carefully to glimpse the men through some gaps in the foliage.

He could see one of them, the man who had tried to break into the key-code doors at the spa. The man looked down, his movements jerky as he did something to his gun.

They were reloading.

"Move!" he whispered to Rachel, and they continued toward the ditch.

It took forever, moving on their bellies through the rows of vines. At one point, one of the men stalked across the end of the row they were cutting through. Edward froze, flattening against the ground.

The man only needed to walk past their row and look down it, and he'd see them.

Edward had to time it right. *Please help us, God.*

The man passed the row to one side of them. As he took the steps past the grapevines that would take him into view of their row, Edward signaled to Rachel, and they slipped through the vine plants back into the row the man had just passed.

They waited for a shout, for a gunshot.

Nothing.

"Go!" he whispered. He leaped to his feet in a low crouch, and they ran down the row away from the man.

They reached the end of the vineyard and paused. There were several yards of open ground before they could slither down into the ditch, open area where the men might see them making a run for it.

He lifted his head quickly, hoping to catch some movement to show where the men were.

Rachel tugged his arm. "One of them is over there." She pointed to a far corner.

He saw a flash of metal—perhaps from the man's gun—on a different side of the vineyard from his partner, but closer to them.

"On three. And move fast. One, two, three!"

They shot out of the vineyard, sprinting as fast as they could while keeping low to the ground. As he reached it, Edward skidded on his hip so he could slide over the edge and into the ditch feet first. He reached up to grab Rachel and pull her in.

The ditch was only four feet deep, so they dropped to their knees among the weeds and grasses and listened.

No shouts. No sounds of movement. No gunshots.

At least, until the men discovered the ditch.

"Go." He pushed her ahead of him down the length of the ditch. It ran almost all the way to a service road near this end of the property. They might be able to flag a car or, at best, make it to the neighboring farm, which had more trees and bushes for cover.

Rachel kept both hands out on either side of her to balance herself against the sides of the ditch as she leaped over clumps of grass while running at an awkward crouch. Edward's knees banged the sides of the ditch at narrow points.

They were almost at the end....

Then they heard a shout. Edward instinctively ducked and threw himself on top of Rachel, expecting a bullet to bury itself in his back.

Then he heard a car horn—and the blast from a shotgun.

Edward tried to twist around to peek behind him down the length of the ditch, but it was too narrow. Rachel was trembling under him. He rose to his knees and peeked over the edge of the ditch.

A rusty pickup truck jostled and rattled over the rough ground directly at the two men, who fired a few shots at the truck. The steel frame seemed to shrug aside the bullets as it barreled toward them. A man in the passenger's seat fired a shotgun at the two intruders—it was one of the farmhands.

The two intruders ran, cutting across the plowed field where the truck would have a harder time following, toward a country road on the other side of the field. They must have a car parked there.

In the distance were two other trucks—Alex's and that of another farmhand. Alex's truck had skidded to a halt near the farmhouse back door, and Alex had already gotten the shotguns from inside and was running toward the two men with a gun in hand. A farmhand followed with the other gun.

The other truck followed the steel monster in pursuit of the two men, although both vehicles stopped at the edge of the plowed field. One man jumped out of the truck and raced after the nearer of the two men.

"Edward!" Alex roared. "Rachel!"

"Here!" Edward scrambled out of the ditch. He reached back to pull out Rachel, and Alex had sprinted around the vineyard by the time Edward got her over the edge onto the grass. Alex and another farmhand helped Edward pull her out completely, as Edward's arms felt like jelly.

He sat on the grass on the side of the ditch, his entire body shaking. The aftereffects of the adrenaline.

Alex's eyes appeared in his vision. "Are you okay?"

"Fine," he managed to gasp. "Not shot."

Rachel turned to Alex. "How did you know?"

"You can thank Jane. She called me."

"Jane?"

"She was working on Naomi's computer. She checked some wires under the desk and found a listening device stuck there."

"What? How did she know what it was?"

"Actually, she sent a photo of it to my cell phone, and I told her it was a bug," Alex admitted. "It looked exactly like the device we found in Naomi's music box. Then Jane remembered that you two had just left, but you'd talked about going to Mama's farm."

And about being alone at the house. And about how Edward intended to call Julio and Chase to meet them there.

"Jane said Naomi was calling you but not getting an answer," Alex said.

"We were already being shot at," Rachel said. "I dropped my phone and we had to leave it."

"I tried calling you," Edward told him.

"I was on the phone with Billy, Grant and Jose," Alex said, nodding to one of them, who stood nearby. "I knew they were in the south field, so I told them to meet me at Mama's house."

"Yeah, who were those two guys?" asked Jose.

Edward shook his head. "We still don't know."

"Hey! Some help, here!" called a voice, and they turned to see Billy and Grant dragging one of the men toward them. They raced to pin him down, Edward following a little slower. Billy ran back to one of the trucks and returned with some rope. In a few minutes, they had bound him up.

"What about the other man?" Alex asked.

"I saw him get away in a blue car heading down Alpine Drive," said Billy, referring to the country road behind the property.

Rachel now got a good look at the man's face and gasped. "You're the one who tried to kill me!"

"No, I didn't!" he blurted.

There was a heartbeat of silence, then the man shook his head at the ground.

"You pointed your gun at me in the restaurant parking lot," Rachel said.

"I never wanted to kill you. It was Lee." The man looked up at Rachel with pleading eyes. "Remember? I hesitated. I didn't shoot."

"You shot at both of us just now," said Edward.

The man shook his head again. "I had a clear shot when you ran toward the vineyard, but I didn't take it. I only started shooting when Lee ran around from the front of the house to head after you."

Rachel's face was pale. "Who hired you to do this?"

He ignored her. "I didn't want anyone dead."

"Who's behind all this?" she persisted.

"You have to tell the police that I hesitated, that I didn't try to kill you," he pleaded.

Alex tried talking to him, but the man shook his head, refusing to say anything more.

"Jane said she'd call the police," Alex told Edward. "They should be here soon, if they don't get lost again."

"Hopefully they remember from the last time they came out here," said Rachel.

"You got here quick, Alex. Were you on the way?"

Alex nodded. "I was only a few minutes away when Jane called."

"Mama's with you? Where is she?" Edward tried

to hurry toward the house, but his legs felt boneless, and he stumbled.

Alex put a hand on his arm to steady him. "I told her to get in the house when I went to get the shotguns."

"Oh, no," Edward replied.

"What?"

"I told Julio and Chase to meet me at the house. It was overheard by that bug when the men found out we were going to be here. When we got here, one of the men was already in the house."

Rachel gasped. "And Julio and Chase never responded when you called for them. Are they all right?"

Carried on the wind, they heard a scream from the house.

Alex took off, along with Jose. The two farmhands holding the man down tensed, but they stayed with him.

Edward grabbed Rachel and they followed Alex. His legs were better, but Rachel's slim frame shook in his arms, and he didn't want to leave her alone.

Mama raced down the back porch steps. Thank goodness, she looked okay.

"Thanks for sending me into a house with two dead bodies inside!" she screamed.

Dead? No, it couldn't be. Julio and Chase were dead?

No, Chase suddenly exited the rear door on wobbly legs, clutching the back of his head.

"Mama," Alex said. "They're not dead."

"Well, I thought they were dead!"

"Where's Julio?" Edward asked Chase as they got closer to the house.

Chase motioned back inside. "He's awake now, but he's not so good. I think they hit him harder than they hit me. He threw up on the living-room floor."

"Oh, no." Mama headed inside to care for Julio.

Chase didn't look as if he should be walking around—he had a huge red bump at the back of his head.

"Sit down," Rachel told him, motioning toward a porch chair. "Hopefully Jane also called the ambulance when she called the police."

The authorities arrived at that moment in a swirling cloud of dust as the cars swerved to a stop in the dirt area in front of and around the house. Detective Carter got out of one of the cars parked to the side of the house, tense and ready, but then relaxed when he saw Edward and Alex standing in the backyard.

"Are you all right, boys?" he asked.

They nodded. Alex gestured toward the vineyard. "Billy and Grant have one of the men tied up."

"I see that," Horatio replied, and Edward turned to see the two farmhands dragging the man between them on the way to the house.

"Why don't you tell me what happened," Horatio said.

Edward and Rachel both told him about being

chased, about Alex rounding up the farmhands and arriving just in time.

"It seems strange that someone would bug Naomi's office instead of yours," said Edward.

"Not really," Rachel said. "Naomi's office is in a separate hallway from the spa rooms, but it's much more accessible than mine, which is behind the card-key-locked doors."

"But what could they have hoped to overhear? Someone's card-key code?" Edward said.

"Regardless, the bug paid off, since they overheard where we would be today."

When Horatio had finished questioning them, he went to find Alex to take his statement. Edward enveloped Rachel in a hug.

She was so small and fragile in his arms. Or maybe she only seemed that way after their flight for their lives today.

"Edward, I knew you'd get us out of it," she murmured into his shoulder. "I knew God would help us."

Before the past few weeks, she'd rarely mentioned God to him. She had never seemed to understand his relationship with God. And now he could see the changes in her—in her words, her actions, even her reactions to the new stresses thrown at her. At them.

Compared to her, he felt tense. One man was captured, but the other was still out there. Rachel was still in danger, although less danger than before.

His mind whirled. What could he do to capture the other man? What could he do to keep Rachel safe from him?

No. He calmed his thoughts.

He remembered the panic that had frozen his brain while in the vineyard. He'd felt helpless. More, he'd felt frustrated that he hadn't been able to keep Rachel safe. His determination to save her had propelled him onward, had propelled his thoughts upward to God.

He'd been so blind to his lack of trust in God. He hadn't trusted God enough before—not with Rachel, not with everything else that had happened.

He had to trust God to take care of them now.

SIXTEEN

As soon as Rachel entered the house, her father wheeled into the foyer and pulled her down into a fierce hug.

"I'm so glad you're all right," he said.

She patted his back. "God was watching over me and Edward, Dad." She'd heard Aunt Becca say things like that before, but she now knew with startling clarity how true it was, how God really had been watching out for her, every moment she was in danger.

He released her. "And one of the men is in custody?"

"His name is Randy," Aunt Becca said. "Horatio says that he's determined Randy will tell us everything soon."

"Rachel, come with me." Dad wheeled back toward his office. "I have something to give to you."

They entered the cool office, the light streaming from the windows casting a golden glow on the wooden floors. Her father reached into a desk drawer and extracted a small jewelry box. He handed it to her.

It was a beautiful marquise-cut ruby ring, set in an old-fashioned setting. It took her breath away.

"It was your grandmother's," Dad said. "I gave it to your mother on our one-year anniversary. She wanted you to have it, since you're the oldest daughter. She told me, 'Give it to her on a really special occasion.'" His mouth twisted. "I kept waiting for just the perfect time. Maybe your high-school graduation...no, that's not special enough. Maybe your college graduation. No, maybe when you got your doctorate. No, your first product launch... Oh, Rach, I'm so sorry." His voice broke.

"Dad." She grasped his shoulder.

"After what you told me when we argued, I realized I was pushing you as if I wanted you to earn this ring. As if your mother wouldn't be pleased enough if I didn't give it to you on *a really special occasion.*" He shook his head. "And today I could have lost you. I would never have told you how proud I am of you."

Tears filled her eyes. "You don't have to tell me, Dad. I've been pushing myself, too. I've been believing a lie."

"If it was a lie, it was a lie I told you," he insisted. "Rachel, honey, I love you very much. Don't ever doubt that."

She reached down to hug him. "I know, Dad." *Now.* "Thank you."

He untangled himself from her to take the ring and slip it on her right hand. "There." He took her hand in his and looked up at her. "And now I can't take you out to dinner. Monica's making me go to bed early. So I want you to go out to dinner with Edward—my treat."

"What? Dad, there's still Randy's partner out there somewhere."

"If I know Horatio Carter, he won't rest until Randy's employer is in custody. And once that happens, the other man still on the loose won't have a reason to keep pursuing you if there's no one to pay him."

He had a point. Randy's employer—the shadowy person or group after Rachel's research and her life— might already be on the run because Randy had been captured and they feared he'd talk. He had no incentive *not* to talk. "We don't even know if Edward is free—"

"I called him on his cell phone while Horatio was driving you home," her father said. He'd apparently already arranged things the way he wanted them. "He actually thinks it's a good idea."

To be honest, the prospect of a few hours with Edward, in a restaurant, had its appeal. And for only ninety minutes or two hours, surrounded by people… surely not much could happen in two hours?

Rachel's favorite restaurant, Danica's Café, was pleasantly crowded that night, but they got a cozy booth along one of the side walls. Rachel supposed it was so that Edward could get a clear view if anyone tried to attack them, but the restaurant was also full of small tables, so a direct attack would be a bit hard.

Then again, what did she know about these things?

One busboy delivered glasses of water while the waiter took their drink orders. Edward ordered coffee, while Rachel asked for her favorite Japanese tea.

When the waiter had left, Edward reached over the table and grasped her hands. "Are you okay? After everything that happened today?"

"Yes." She squeezed his hand. "I'm glad I had you to keep me safe."

He shook his head. "I was afraid, Rach. I was leading you through the vineyard and into the ditch, but I was afraid I was only going to get us killed."

"I knew you wouldn't." He opened his mouth to protest, but she interrupted him. "I knew you wouldn't because through it all, I felt God's presence with me again."

His eyes were dark as they stared at her. "I had a hard time trusting Him in the midst of all that."

She smiled reassuringly at him. "It was almost as if He were whispering to me to trust Him, so I did. And for the first time in my life, I realized that God had His hand over us completely, even in the midst of those terrible twenty minutes. That He had His hand over everything, because everything is His."

She stared at the ruby ring on her finger. "You know I don't normally read my Bible very consistently, but I've been reading it more lately. And as I crawled through the grapevines, the Bible verse I had read that morning flashed through my mind—'The earth is the Lord's and everything in it.' God had control over everything, so I could keep my attention focused on your instructions and not on my own feelings of panic."

They were interrupted by her steaming pot of tea and a teacup, but Edward didn't relinquish her hand, simply shifted them to the side, his thumb caressing her knuckles.

"I haven't been trusting God enough," he confessed. "Not with my life and work. Not with your life."

"God has been protecting me, all this time. I know that now."

"I didn't know about your relationship with your dad, and I just backed away from you. I know I hurt you by doing that."

"Oh, Edward, you were reacting out of hurt. Your mother told me about your papa."

"You needed someone in your corner—you needed a friend just when things were getting stressful with your dad and the research. I wasn't there for you then, but I'm here for you now, and I won't leave you again."

"You didn't exactly move across the state or anything like that."

He gave a half smile.

Just then the waiter slipped Edward's coffee onto the table. "Oh," the waiter said, hefting a pot of tea but seeing Rachel's pot already in front of her. "I'll be right back to take your order." He left.

Edward sipped his coffee, then grimaced. "It's

cold." He looked up to flag the waiter, but he had already disappeared.

Rachel had poured a cup of her tea, so she shoved it toward him. "Want some?"

He looked at her cup as if she'd offered him poison. "I had green tea once. It was nasty and bitter. It was also bright green like antifreeze."

She laughed. "That was probably *matcha,* which is the tea used in the Japanese Tea Ceremony. Not everyone likes it. This is *genmaicha,* which is a lighter green tea with toasted rice."

"Rice? In tea?"

"It's good. Try it."

He took a sip, then made a horrible face as he swallowed. "It's really bitter."

"It is?" She smelled it. It did have a strange bitter smell. "I'll ask for another pot. Dad always says I'm too picky about my tea—"

"We should figure out what we want to eat, or we'll be out too late." Edward opened his menu, but his eyes twinkled over the edge. "I promised your father to have you back before midnight."

"I'm not going to turn into a pumpkin. And I'm not a teenager." But then she embarrassed herself with a yawn.

"A good night's sleep will be good for both of us. Tomorrow we'll be able to figure out what we're going to do next."

The restaurant was busy, and after ten minutes the waiter paused by their table with an armload of entrées to apologize for the wait and promise to be back in a few minutes to take their order. Rachel didn't mind—she took that time to tell Edward about her conversation with her father and the ring, which he admired.

The waiter finally returned with profuse apologies.

After Rachel ordered another pot of tea and lasagna, Edward glanced up from his menu. "Can you... can..." A strange spasm crossed his face. He blinked, rubbing a hand across his cheeks, his jaw, his mouth. "Sorry about that. Can you tell me what the soup is tonight?"

"Baked potato—creamy potato soup with cheddar cheese, green onions and bacon."

Rachel perked up. "Oh, I'll have a cup of that."

Edward looked strangely at her. "Lasagna and baked potato soup?" he asked, then his knee jerked, popping her in the kneecap.

"Ow."

"Sorry." His brow furrowed. "I don't know why I did that. My legs are antsy."

He ordered rotisserie chicken and a salad, then added, "And I'd like..."

Suddenly Rachel noticed that strange spasm across his facial muscles again, and his neck arched for a moment.

"...a fresh cup of coffee. This one's cold."

"Oh, I'm sorry," the waiter said, his neck coloring. He whisked away Edward's cup.

"Edward, are you—" Her breath caught.

He had turned pale, and was blinking rapidly. There was another spasm across his face. Another strange jerk of his legs, arching of his neck, stiffness across his shoulders. Then he collapsed onto the floor.

"Edward!" She dropped to the ground next to him. At first she thought he was having a seizure, but then she realized that his muscle spasms and rigidity were different from the seizures she'd seen and treated when she did her medical-school residency. "Edward!"

She became aware that other diners had gotten up and gathered around them. "Someone call an ambulance!"

Her medical training, even though it had been years ago, came rushing back to her. She shoved aside empty chairs to clear the area around his body and then rolled him onto his side. His skin was clammy under her fingers.

Oh, please, God, help him…!

She had just talked to him about God being with her. She had felt His presence earlier today.

The earth is the Lord's, and everything in it.

Please, God, only You can save him now. You hold everything in Your hands. Even Edward.

And something deep inside her, something that defied logic, that spoke louder than her panicked thoughts, told her that God was here with her, no matter what happened.

No matter what happened.

Lord, You are everything.

"Miss? I'm a paramedic," said a deep voice at her shoulder.

She immediately moved aside and let the man look at Edward.

A woman who had been sitting at the booth next to them put her arm around Rachel. "It'll be okay."

The paramedic's body kneeling over Edward blocked her view of his face. What was happening? She had a medical degree and a Ph.D. in dermatology, and yet she was helpless. *Oh, Edward.*

Her thumb pressed the ruby ring into her finger painfully.

"Thank you for calling the ambulance," she told the woman. She had seen her whipping out her cell phone.

The woman shook her head. "I didn't need to. This man was sitting at that table over there." She pointed to a table and chairs a few feet away. "He'd just gotten off his shift and he happened to have his gear with him. You're very lucky, dear."

A paramedic who *happened* to be here? With his gear?

Thank You, Lord.

The restaurant manager stepped into the circle around Edward. "Give him some space," he said, and restaurant patrons backed up to give them some air.

"Miss?" The manager turned to her. "What happened?"

"I don't know…" She glanced at the table. "My tea. He drank my tea."

Suddenly a fist closed tight over her heart. Edward had drunk the tea meant for her.

Their waiter had a shocked look on his face. "I didn't give you that tea," he protested. "You already had it when I came with your order."

She thought back. He *hadn't* brought it to them. The busboy who had given her the tea had been a much larger man…but she couldn't remember more than that. She hadn't even looked up at him because she'd been so focused on Edward.

"He was a tall man," she stammered. "The busboy who gave me the tea."

"Tall?" The manager looked confused. "We only have one tall waiter." He pointed to a thin, gangly young man with a shocking crop of red curls.

"No, the busboy was…big." Bigger than that man.

Big like the man who had attacked Edward in the parking lot that night?

Who had brought her the tea? Had they been trying to kill her?

And would they kill Edward now instead?

God was so much bigger than she'd ever conceived. And yet He'd been there for her.

And for Edward.

She knew He would continue to be there for her,

even though the threat against her was getting worse and impacting the people she loved.

She trusted God, but she also wasn't being stupid and taking unnecessary chances—she sat in the hospital waiting room in full view of the nurses' station, and she had made sure they all knew she was waiting for news about Edward and for his family and hers to arrive.

She didn't like the sheer number of people bustling around the waiting area, but she still felt the vestiges of uneasiness about being alone out in the open— remnants of the pursuit from this afternoon. So the press of the crowd in the hospital didn't unnerve her the way it normally would.

But she stayed alert, on edge. Until someone she trusted came to be with her, she felt exposed and vulnerable without Edward near her.

Her raw nerves made her jittery, so she sat in the stiff plastic chair and tried to calm herself with prayer, clenching her hands together so tightly that the marquise-cut ruby ring made an indentation in her skin. The words had a hard time coming.

How was Edward doing? The paramedic had told her that he thought Edward had been poisoned, but that since it appeared he didn't drink much of the tea, his symptoms were relatively minor. He'd done what he could. Someone had apparently called the ambulance—one that was on call—which had arrived only minutes later to whisk Edward and her to the hospital. The off-duty paramedic had ridden to the hospital with Rachel and told her that the doctors would have more information once they examined and treated him. Since arriving, she hadn't seen the paramedic or Edward.

The paramedic's reassurances prevented her from being as crazed with worry as she would have been right now, but she still wanted news of him.

And yet, God had taken care of him. What were the odds that a paramedic would have been at that restaurant, just off his shift, and still having all his gear with him? Those first few minutes when the paramedic had worked on Edward might have saved his life.

God had saved his life.

Thank You, God.

She had to trust that God would still have control over everything now.

She remembered the stars she saw with Alex and Edward the other night. God had revealed His character to her that night, and ever since.

Now she had to show Him who she was—if she was going to trust in what He showed her or not.

The earth is the Lord's, and everything in it.

Everything—including Edward. Including her relationship with her father. Including her product launch. Including her life.

Lord, everything in my life is Yours. Everything.

It was as if chains had been wrapped around her shoulders, around her heart, and they were suddenly lifted away. God was all she needed to trust in. He was all she would ever need.

Lord, You are everything.

It would all be okay.

"Rachel."

Detective Carter's concerned voice cut through her thoughts and prayers, and she leaped to her feet. He strode through the waiting room crowd, his demeanor exuding enough authority to make people give way for him, and yet his eyes on her were filled with kindness.

"How are you doing?" he said, his hand briefly touching her elbow.

"I'm fine." She could barely get the words out. She was so relieved to see him. "You got here fast."

"I left the station as soon as I got your phone call. How's Edward?"

"I don't know yet. The doctors haven't talked to me. The paramedic said he thinks Edward will be okay because he didn't drink much of the poison."

His brow furrowed. "Yes, on the phone you mentioned something about tea?"

She stifled the sob that rose in her throat. "He drank some tea that I had ordered, that was meant for me."

"You didn't drink any of it?"

"No."

"Tell me everything." He took out his notebook and wrote as she recounted what happened. "And you haven't heard from any of the doctors yet about Edward?" he asked as he closed his notebook.

"No."

"Wait here." He walked a few steps to talk to the nurses at the station, and one left through the double doors into the hospital. "I asked them to get a doctor," he told Rachel when he came back to her.

"Thank you."

"Did you call Edward's family?"

"Yes. I called mine, too."

"I'll stay with you until they get here. It's not safe for you to be here alone," he added, with a discreet glance around the waiting area as he took the seat next to hers.

She gave him a grateful smile as she sat back down again. His stalwart presence helped her lungs relax so she could breathe easier. "I thought that the other man would lay low for a while after you arrested his partner—what's his name—Randy?"

Detective Carter nodded.

"Has he said anything about who hired him?"

The detective shook his head. "Not yet. But don't worry, Rachel." He gave her a comforting smile. "He will. I'll make sure of it." His promise, given in his gravelly voice, held a ring of determination.

"Maybe the other man will stop trying to get to me once Randy talks." She had to remain positive about this or she might start screaming in the middle of the waiting room.

"I will find the people responsible for all this,"

Detective Carter told her. "You can trust me to not rest until I find them."

"Did you already talk to the people at the restaurant?"

He nodded. "Briefly. I stopped there before I came here to find you. I have other officers still there taking statements." Suddenly, his cell phone rang. "Hello?"

At the same moment, a male nurse in scrubs came toward the two of them. "You're here waiting to see Edward Villa?"

"Yes." Rachel shot to her feet. "Is he okay?"

"The doctor is with him now, but he says you can come into his room to see him."

Rachel looked to Detective Carter. The phone call had propelled him to his feet and given alertness to his face and his voice. "Yes, put him through." He then nodded to Rachel. "Go ahead, I'll be right behind you."

Rachel followed the nurse through the doors. A couple of male nurses had helped bring Edward into the hospital, and she remembered the emergency-room doctor who had met them, a young Indian man.

This nurse looked familiar, and yet…she couldn't quite place him among all the people she'd seen upon arriving here.

They passed through the double doors, with Detective Carter still in the waiting area although slowly following them as he talked on his cell phone.

And then, a few feet down the busy hospital hallway, she remembered where she'd seen the man.

In a dark restaurant parking lot, struggling with Edward.

She stumbled and groped at the wall. She had no air in her lungs to scream. Spinning around, she tried to rush back toward the doors.

A beefy arm gripped her around the waist, pinning one of her arms to her side, but she wriggled the other one loose. He overshadowed her, blocking her view of the other people rushing around the hallway, and blocking their view as he clapped a cloth over her nose and mouth.

"Miss, are you all right?" he said in questioning tones, belying his menacing grip over her mouth.

Her vision spun. She clawed at his arm around her, but he wouldn't let go. In the distance, she heard his mock-concerned voice, "Miss? What's wrong?" for the benefit of the other nurses and doctors around them.

Surely someone would notice what he was doing. Surely someone…

And then everything went black.

SEVENTEEN

Rachel awoke slowly to a headache pounding pain-fully against her forehead. To the muffled sound of a deep voice in the distance. To the smell of stagnant water, drowned weeds, rotting insects.

She cracked her eyes open, but the light blinded her and stabbed painfully into her skull. She wanted to just sit here and wait for the headache to recede.

Then she remembered. The man. The cloth over her mouth. Edward.

She forced her eyes open, her brain screaming at the pain of the light piercing her eyeballs. Then her vision came into focus, and she started to feel her limbs.

She sat in a car. In the driver's seat. Her hands duct-taped to the steering wheel. Duct tape over her mouth.

It was still nighttime, and the car was parked facing a pond, tilted down the sloping bank so that the light from the headlights reflected off the dirty water.

She knew this place. It was old Mr. Rivers's farm, just off the highway. Run-down, a constant topic of debate among his neighbors who objected to the eyesore sitting smack-dab in the middle of their well-tended vineyards and fields. The rank smell from the large pond on his property made the tourists shorten their wine tasting visits at the vineyards next door and not return.

The pond was deep. No one came near because of the smell.

She'd drown here and no one would find her body.

No! She had to stay calm. She had to find a way out of this.

How? There was duct tape wrapped around the steering wheel, her wrists and up her hands, partially covering her knuckles, immobilizing her arms. How was she supposed to escape from this?

Her breathing came in short gasps. Her vision began to cloud.

No, she couldn't pass out now. She had to calm down. Breathe. Breathe. Think.

God was with her.

God, help me....

Movement at the corner of her eye. She glanced up into the rearview mirror and saw dimly the edge of a man's head in the darkness. She slowly adjusted her head and her field of vision to see him better.

The man from the parking lot, the male nurse at the hospital, stood several yards behind the car, talking on his cell phone. Then, still talking, he began to walk along the side of the car toward the driver's side window.

She shut her eyes and tried to relax her face. She sagged against the seat belt and the duct tape, hoping to look like deadweight and still unconscious.

"Yeah, she's still out."

Then, she heard the person he was talking to—a female speaking loud enough that her voice carried through the earpiece of the phone for Rachel to barely make it out in the quiet, but not enough to distinguish what she was saying.

While he was listening, she heard him rustle in his jacket pocket. She barely cracked an eye and saw he was in her field of vision but partially turned away from her.

Then he did something curious—he removed another cell phone from his pocket and tossed it into the weeds at the edge of the pond, along with another small object—she thought it might have been the phone's battery, but she wasn't sure.

"Mmm-hmm." He turned and walked back up the bank of the pond, away from the car.

She tugged at her hands, hoping the duct tape was loose or could be loosened, but it held her fast.

Think. Think.

She cast a glance around the car, squinting in the dim light. Next to her on the passenger seat was her purse. She had her cell phone inside, her house keys… but she couldn't reach any of it.

She twisted her hands, hoping the torque would free

her. The edges of the tape cut into her skin, leaving a thin red line of blood.

But the tape didn't shift.

Then the first rays of the morning sun cleared the horizon in the distance, gilding the steering wheel. She had been out for longer than she thought if it was already dawn.

And something glittered.

The gold of the ring her father had given her. It had shifted so that the ruby faced her palm, and the man had forgotten to remove it.

She worked her thumb—it was loose. She arced her fingers away from the steering wheel so she could work her thumb over the ruby and rotate the ring on her finger. Just a few centimeters more...

The marquis-cut ruby cleared her fingers and was now exposed.

She glanced in the rearview mirror. Illuminated in the small taillights on the car, the man's back was still toward her.

She leaned forward and tried to use the edge of the ruby to puncture the duct tape over her lips. If she could free her mouth...

A soft tear. Quiet ripping. She worked the ring over the tape until she could open her mouth and use her teeth.

She leaned farther forward and attacked the duct tape on her hands. She often used duct tape in the lab to tie together hoses or flasks, and while she knew her dentist hated it, she usually used her teeth to tear off pieces.

The tape was wrapped around her hand several times, so she worked each layer, tugging, shredding, pulling with her teeth as a long jagged line began to form down the duct tape.

And then one hand was free.

The man's voice started to get louder. "Okay, fine." The click of him closing his cell phone.

She darted a look at the rearview mirror and saw him approaching the car.

Oh, no! Would he see the torn tape on her hand, her mouth? She repositioned her hand on the steering wheel and turned her head slightly away from the window. Hopefully he wouldn't look too closely.

But he didn't even approach the driver's side of the car. Instead, the car rocked forward—one, two, three times, each movement more forceful.

On the fourth time, she heard him grunt at the back of his throat, and the car slowly rolled forward.

The car hit resistance when the water sloshed against the front end, but the slope of the bank, the car's momentum and the man's persistent strength pushed the car forward, inch by inch.

It took all her strength to remain motionless as the man continued to push at the car. Her nerves were shrieking at her to do something as rivulets of water punctured the edge of the car door and soaked the floor. She swallowed a scream as she saw the water of the pond rise up on the outside of the car door until it reached the bottom of the open window and spilled over into her lap. She gagged. It smelled like dead frogs.

If she didn't keep her head, *she* would be dead.

The man sloshed through the water as he pushed the car deeper into the pond. Finally, he gave one last huge shove.

She frantically watched the rearview mirror. The man stood knee-deep in water, watching the car sink. If he saw that she was now awake, he gave no sign.

He turned and splashed out of the water, back onto the bank.

Rachel jerked her body forward and started tearing at the duct tape on her other hand with her teeth and her freed hand. She tasted the pond water but her panic kept her doggedly working. She wasn't completely helpless—she already had one hand loose. She had to survive.

The water climbed up her nose. She squeezed her eyes shut and kept working. The tape was tearing in short pieces. She twisted her hand, and the water added lubrication. The level rose above her ears, and she only heard the dark silence of the water.

And then another inch of duct tape ripped and she could pull her hand free. She shoved her head upward and found a slim crack of air between the ceiling and the surface, rapidly shrinking. She took a deep breath, then went under again.

She fumbled with her seat belt, clicked it. Nothing. She clicked it again and again.

Please, God.

The seat belt unlatched.

Cell phone.

The thought came out of nowhere, but she cracked her eyes open under the murky water and fumbled on the passenger seat for her purse.

There was nothing on the seat.

She bent and dived her hand down to the floor, sweeping the carpet—there. She ripped the bag open and dug through until her fingers touched the rubbery outside of her phone.

She untangled her hand from the bag and twisted to grab the edge of the open window. She looked upward and saw the lightening sky through the water. She wasn't far from the surface.

Was the man watching the car sink?

She pulled herself through the water out of the car, careful not to break the surface, hoping the green water hid the sight of her escaping. She spun in the water and dived deeper, but away from the car, away from the bank where the man might still be standing.

Her lungs were painfully tight in her chest, but she kept swimming, her hand locked around her cell phone. She skimmed over weeds near the bottom of the pond which might trap her.

And then she felt sloping slime, and followed it upward, pulling her body along. The water seemed darker here on this side of the pond.

She tried not to break the surface too quickly, but

her aching lungs made her gasp softly as her mouth cleared the water. She turned to look back.

The dropping branches of a tree filled her vision—a tree growing near the bank had tilted, and its dead branches with a few clinging leaves draped over the water, partially obscuring her from view. She shifted to see around the branches toward the opposite bank.

The man was walking across the field toward where she knew the highway lay. Possibly to be picked up there by the woman he'd been talking to.

He didn't know she'd escaped. He didn't know she was alive.

Until today, Rachel had never before been thankful that she was a klutz. But if she hadn't already destroyed two other cell phones by spilling chemicals on them in the lab or answering them before taking off her gloves, then a few months ago she would never have gotten the latest super-rugged cell phone, which also happened to be waterproof.

She shivered while sitting on the sodden bank under the tilting tree and flipped open her phone. It lit up. *Thank You, God.* She dialed.

"Rachel!" Detective Carter practically shouted into the phone. "Are you all right?"

"I'm fine," she said, although it came out a bit muffled because her teeth were chattering. "I'm at Mr. Rivers's pond. The man who attacked Edward tried to drown me."

"Is he still there?"

"No, I think he's gone. I saw him walking toward the highway. He had been talking to a woman on his cell phone. And, Detective? I don't think he knows I survived."

"I understand. I'll be right there."

"Please h-hurry," she stammered. "It's cold."

He arrived with Aunt Becca, Naomi and Monica, as well as an ambulance. They arrived in unmarked police cars, presumably so they wouldn't attract attention while driving through town and on the highway, since Rachel's attacker didn't know she wasn't dead.

At first, when the cars turned off the highway and approached the pond, Rachel worried that they were more thugs sent by whoever that man's employer was. Then the detective rushed out of one of the cars, followed by Aunt Becca and her sisters.

"I was so worried," her aunt said as she was smothered in her embrace. Naomi and Monica joined them in a group hug.

Enfolded by her family, Rachel felt her eyes well up and she buried her stuffed nose in Aunt Becca's woolen car coat. Their bodies pressed in on her like a warm comforter.

As they released her, she wiped her eyes, and Detective Carter clasped her shoulder in a gentle grip. "I'm so sorry, Rachel. I was only a few seconds behind you, but it was enough."

"He took me out with formaldehyde," she said. "I recognized the smell because I use it in the lab."

"Just before he came out to the waiting area, I got a phone call—do you remember that?"

She nodded.

"Someone had called the police station saying they had information on Edward's poisoning, and they wanted to speak to me. That's why I said I'd be right behind you. But when the caller was connected to me, the line was dead. He'd hung up." His brows came down over his gray eyes. "I think the caller was the man who kidnapped you. He needed to distract me so he could separate us."

"How did he get me out of the hospital?" By now, a paramedic had wrapped a blanket around her and was checking her vitals.

"We're not sure. I asked the nurses, and they said they'd seen a woman faint and a male nurse carry her into a room. But when I went there, the room was empty."

"Did you trace the call?"

"It was from a cell phone, and the signal went dead."

Then she remembered. "The man was talking on a cell phone, but then he threw a second cell phone and maybe the battery near the pond." She pointed to the general area, and the detective barked orders to a few policemen to search for it.

"Now, tell me what happened," Detective Carter said.

Rachel described waking up in the car, tearing

through the duct tape, swimming from the drowning car and seeing the man walking away.

"You said the man was talking on his cell phone to a woman?"

"I think it was a woman. When I heard the pitch of the voice I thought it was a woman. But I couldn't hear well enough to understand what she was saying or to recognize if I knew her."

"We'll examine the discarded cell phone and get a tow truck to get the car out of the pond," the detective said. "We also have been talking to the man we arrested, Randy, and his lawyer. We have hopes he'll cooperate soon."

"Horatio, you have to protect her," Aunt Becca told him. "Now that Edward's in the hospital—"

"How is he?"

"We didn't see him, but we spoke to his brother and mother last night at the hospital," Naomi said. "The doctors said that he was poisoned with strychnine, but since he only drank a little of the tea, and because that paramedic was at the restaurant to treat him right away, he'll be fine. They'll release him in a few days."

Thank You, Lord.

Monica had been talking to the paramedic who had examined Rachel, and she now put an arm around her sister. "They've cleared you to go. Let's get you home and put you in a hot shower."

"Dad was frantic," said Naomi. "When we arrived at the hospital last night and you were missing, we had to tell him, and I've never seen him so upset. He asked all of us to stay up with him last night praying for you."

"Dad did that?" Rachel had never known her father to be so open about his faith.

"God heard our prayers," Aunt Becca said, and she drew close to Rachel's side to give her a squeeze. "Praise Jesus, He kept you safe."

"Yes, He did."

The earth is the Lord's, and everything in it.

EIGHTEEN

Edward had never felt so vulnerable and exposed as he did lying in that hospital bed. At the same time, he fought the burning in his chest to get up, get dressed and do what he could to protect Rachel.

A snore came from the corner. Alex sat rumpled in the chair, asleep. After arriving at the hospital and discovering Rachel was missing, Alex had immediately gone out to find any contacts he had who might be able to help find her. Once she'd called Detective Carter early this morning, Alex had come back to the hospital and collapsed in a tired heap.

But Rachel was still in danger. That man was still after her. The identity of whoever hired him was still a mystery.

And Edward lay in a cotton gown in a hospital bed, his body weak and strangely aching, as if he'd worked all day in the fields at the farm.

That had been some sip of tea.

Alex's snores grew in volume, and Mama, who had been reading out loud from her Bible, sighed and shut the book. "He is shamefully drowning out the words of God."

Edward laughed, although it hurt his stomach. "He was up all night, trying to find Rachel. He didn't get back here until almost eight this morning." Edward had learned that when Detective Carter had called to tell Alex that Rachel was okay, Alex had been almost two hours away up north, following a lead from a friend who was a trucker. He'd turned around, but it had taken him a while to get back to Sonoma.

"Praise the Lord she's all right," Mama said.

"She's still not safe, Mama."

His mother's dark eyes were reproachful. "Jesus saved her from being drowned. Don't you think He'll continue to watch over her?"

He hadn't thought of that.

"You have been antsy. And it's not a good kind of antsy, either. I think that what you're feeling is more about you than it is about her."

More about him...?

No, Mama didn't understand. Edward needed to be feeling better, to be up and out of this bed. He shouldn't have taken her to that restaurant in the first place—he'd been too complacent once that man Randy had been captured. He should have been more alert. He should have been... He should have done...

"What are you thinking about?" His mama's gentle admonishment cut through the noise in his brain. "It's distracting you from God's voice."

Distractions. Her words convicted him, even through all the recriminations in his head. Senseless noise. They drained him even more than the poison had, leaving him empty.

His thoughts were distractions, ripping into him, tearing him into a million pieces.

He needed to put the pieces back in place.

He needed *God* to put the pieces back in place.

Lately, he hadn't been trusting God enough. And despite realizing that, here he was, *still* not trusting Him enough.

Lord, I'm just too scattered right now. I'm empty. I'm weak. I'm...broken.

Had he been trying to be Superman, trying too hard in the face of all the troubles facing Rachel?

Slowly, the pieces fell into place again. *Lord, I lift all these things up to You.*

That's all he needed to say. It's all his heart needed to say.

Rachel surprised him by coming to the hospital early that afternoon. Her smile as she saw him made the imprisoning hospital room suddenly feel like a brightly sunlit field.

She embraced him, smelling strongly of lavender and citrus, as if she'd taken a fresh shower. "I'm so glad you're okay," she said.

"Ditto."

"Hi, Carmella, Alex." She gave his mama a hug, and Alex bussed her cheek. "I'd have been here sooner, but I needed to wash the pond water out of my hair. I smelled like a sewer." She sat in the chair next to his bed.

He teasingly tweaked her chin. "After what you told me on the phone, I half expected you to smell like a rotting fish."

She made a face. "Don't even joke about that."

"I wasn't expecting you here so early. You should be resting."

"So should you."

He rolled his eyes. "I've been resting all day."

She took his hand. "I didn't want to be away from you."

He ran his calloused fingers over her smooth ones, feeling new cuts in her hand. "From the duct tape?" She'd told him what happened over the phone earlier that day.

"It doesn't hurt." She squeezed his hand. "I'm just glad you're okay."

If he'd drunk more of that tea... If the paramedic hadn't been there...God had been taking care of him, as well as Rachel. "Did your family come with you?"

"Aunt Becca is, uh...taking extraordinarily long to park the car."

"Actually, I ran into Horatio in the parking garage," Rachel's aunt Becca said as she walked in. She smiled at Edward, but her eyes were serious. So was the face of Detective Carter, who followed her into the room.

"Naomi drove separately because she had to stop in

at the spa first," Becca said. "She'll be here in a few minutes. She'll probably kill us, but I want to hear what Horatio found out."

"News?" Edward asked Horatio.

Horatio nodded. "Randy, the man you captured, confessed in exchange for a lighter sentence."

Mama *hmphed*. "Lighter sentence? Doing community service? Send him to my farm—I'll put him to work."

"Not community service," Horatio assured her.

"So who hired him?" Rachel asked.

"Gloria Reynolds."

"What?" Rachel shot to her feet.

Becca echoed her cry. "Our spa client, Gloria Reynolds?"

Horatio nodded grimly.

"But...I just saw her this morning at the spa!" Becca's voice rose in a wail.

"You did?" Horatio went on alert. "When?"

"After we dropped Rachel off at home to shower, one of the receptionists called about an aesthetician who was accidentally double booked, so Naomi and I went back to the spa. I was at the appointment desk when I saw her walk in."

"Was she supposed to be there?"

"Gloria Reynolds has booked several appointments for the past few days, one or two every day. So when she came in today, I didn't think anything of it," Becca moaned. "She didn't have an appointment today, but I thought perhaps she'd come to collect something she left behind in the women's bathroom from her appointment a couple days ago. She pays the fee for the spa's Tamarind membership, which means she can use the Tamarind women's lounge anytime she likes. She left after only a few minutes."

"So you didn't speak to her?"

Becca shook her head. "But maybe Naomi saw her or spoke to her." She took out her cell phone. "I'll text her and ask her to hurry up and get here."

"What else did Randy tell you?" Edward asked Horatio.

"The name of the other man is Lee," Horatio said. "Randy said he and Lee have partnered together several times. Lee is the muscle, Randy is the tech."

"So it was Randy who dismantled the security system in my greenhouse."

"And that's why he was the one at the spa, trying to break into the card-key lock," Becca said.

"Gloria had told Randy and Lee to steal a few basil plants and destroy the rest—to sabotage your product launch," Horatio told Rachel. "But Edward interrupted them before they could finish the job. They also didn't realize that just tossing the plants around wouldn't kill them, especially since Edward was able to move and replant them so quickly afterward."

"Don't give Edward all the glory," Alex said from the corner with a yawn. "I helped replant all those basil."

"Hush," Mama said, with a shake to Alex's shoulder.

"Randy said that once Gloria had the plants, she ordered them to kill you, which was why they tried to run you down on your bike. But then after that, she told them that she also needed the scar-reduction-cream formulation in addition to the plants."

"That explains a lot," said Rachel. "I wondered why they'd tried to run me off the road, since my death at that point wouldn't enable them to get the formulation data. She apparently changed her mind, which was why they tried to get into the spa after that."

"They were the ones who stole the laptop, thinking it was Rachel's. When they realized it had nothing on it, they returned it with a GPS tracker in the case, but they didn't realize until Randy tried to steal it in San Francisco that it was Naomi's computer and not yours."

"So that confirms why he just ran away without the laptop," Rachel said.

"Randy also confessed to sneaking into your room at the house when Lee rang the doorbell as the fake UPS deliveryman," Horatio said. "They had hoped you'd have your research data on your computer at home."

Rachel shook her head. "It was all on my computer at work."

"That means it was Gloria who bribed Stephanie to steal the formula," Becca said.

Horatio nodded. "Randy said that Gloria called him to tell him to kill Rachel because she had gotten the formula."

"It would make sense," said Rachel slowly. "Once I was out of the way, Gloria could take as much time as she wanted to develop her scar-reduction cream. Even with the formulation and a freelance cosmetics lab already set up and ready to go, she'd still need several months to verify the formulation and grow the number of mature basil plants that she would need."

"She was eliminating the competition." Becca put an arm around Rachel.

"Randy told me that he hadn't wanted to kill me," Rachel said to Horatio. "Does he still insist that's true?"

He nodded. "He says that's why he didn't shoot you in the restaurant parking lot. Lee apparently has no qualms, which is why he tried to poison your tea and then kidnapped you to make you disappear."

"Why that elaborate scenario to drown me? Why not just shoot me?"

Her callous way of discussing it made Edward wince.

Alex opened his mouth as if to answer her, then glanced at Mama and Becca and shut his mouth.

But Rachel saw the motion. "What?"

Alex hesitated.

"Just tell me."

"It's less messy," Alex said. "Your body in a stolen car, sitting in a pond for who knows how long. Any evidence would be gone. And the police wouldn't definitely know, right away, that you were dead."

"It would probably have initially changed our search tactics," Horatio admitted.

"Did you arrest Gloria Reynolds?" Becca asked.

Horatio's mouth formed a frustrated line. "She's been missing for a couple days already."

"But I saw her this morning," Becca protested.

"She apparently discovered Randy had been arrested—possibly from Lee—and she left her house soon after we took Randy into custody. Her husband says she hasn't been home since."

"Surely her husband knew what she was doing, or else why didn't he report her missing?" Becca's eyes sparked.

"He says he thought she had gone to her sister's place for a few days. He also says he didn't know where she'd gotten the scar-reduction-cream formula."

"Well, what *does* he know?"

"Two years ago, she had commissioned a cosmetics lab to make some diamond-dust cleanser—"

"This proves she lied to us and did hire Steve Schmidt to steal it off my computer," Rachel cried. "Did Randy confess to killing Steve, too?"

"He insists Lee did it, and that he wasn't there when it happened. Ms. Reynolds wasn't very smart about that cleanser." A smile hovered around the edges of Horatio's mouth as he said it. "She simply gave it to several of her husband's diamond clients to try."

Rachel gasped. "That formula was terrible. It didn't even go into clinical trials—my experiments indicated it would cause scarring."

Horatio nodded grimly. "Those clients are apparently threatening to go public with their experiences, although they haven't yet filed lawsuits, which is why no one knew about Gloria's moonlighting in cosmetics. The negative press of legal actions might cause public ruin for Mr. Reynolds's reputation as a diamond businessman."

"But what does that have to do with Rachel's scar-reduction-cream formula now?" Becca asked.

"Among the research notes Steve stole, I had made mention of ideas about a scar-reduction cream made from a basil plant extract," Rachel answered her. "If Gloria simply gave all the files to the cosmetics lab, they would have had those notes. All Gloria would need to do is find out that I hired Edward to grow basil plants, and the lab would know that's the project I'm pursuing for our spring product launch. But the lab had the wrong basil plant species name."

"Her husband said that the lab she's working with hadn't met with any success on the new cream. Gloria had her hopes pinned on that cream because if it worked, it would stop the threatened lawsuits against the Reynoldses and even be a testimony to the efficacy of the cream. It also would become a hot new product the Reynoldses could market," Horatio continued.

"The lab must have suspected they had the wrong species of basil, so she had those men steal the basil from Edward's greenhouse," Rachel said. "But in order to catch up to my production timeline, the lab needed the formulation, too."

"Mr. Reynolds insists he didn't know his wife had acquired those formulations illegally," Horatio said. "Right now, I have no evidence against him, just against Ms. Reynolds."

"Are you sure he doesn't know where Gloria is?"

Horatio shook his head. "I have an all-points bulletin out on her, and Randy has given us information on how to find and capture Lee."

The detective turned to Rachel. "Until we have her and Lee, you need to stay low. Neither of them knows you survived Lee's last attempt on your life, so let's keep it that way."

"Who doesn't know you survived?" Naomi asked as she rushed into Edward's hospital room. "I can't believe you started without me. Aunt Becca said there was something urgent?"

"Gloria Reynolds is the person trying to kill Rachel," Becca told her.

Naomi's mouth dropped open. "Our spa client? Gloria was the one talking to Rachel's kidnapper on the phone?"

"She's apparently been missing for days, ever since Randy was captured—"

"But she walked into the spa this morning," Naomi burst out.

"I saw her," Becca said excitedly. "Did you talk to her?"

Naomi nodded, her eyes unfocused, her face white. "Oh, no."

Edward had a sinking feeling in his gut.

"Gloria sought me out and said she hadn't seen Rachel recently, asked if she was okay." Naomi's brow wrinkled in dismay. "I said you were fine. Because by then, I knew were."

Horatio frowned. "She'd probably been hoping you'd give away if you were lying and still worried about Rachel."

"And I would have. If Rachel were still missing, there's no way I could have hidden that from anyone."

"What was her reaction?"

"I don't know," Naomi said, chewing her bottom lip. "I didn't pay much attention to her. I was giving instructions to two massage therapists and only took a second to answer her." She gave a frustrated huff. "I should have been paying attention. Gloria never asks about any of the family when she comes to the spa."

"Do you remember anything else she said?"

"She didn't say anything else to me," Naomi replied. "But maybe she spoke to one of the other staff...."

"I'll get on it." Horatio pulled out his cell phone.

"I should have known," Naomi whispered hoarsely. "Gloria looked less...made-up than normal. A little antsy. And I didn't even suspect anything was wrong."

"I didn't even notice her appearance, and I saw her

enter and leave," Becca said. "I just let her walk right out of the spa."

"Even if you had suspected her, she'd have been able to leave faster than you could call a security guard or the police," said Rachel.

"But, Rach, now she knows." Naomi gripped her sister's shoulders. "Gloria Reynolds knows you're still alive."

NINETEEN

With everything she had endured, it somehow felt wrong that her life was still in danger. When would all this end?

Rachel grabbed her house keys and found Naomi in the kitchen. "Can I borrow your winter coat?"

"Where's yours?"

"Alex found a GPS tracker shoved in the lining. That's how Gloria's goons found me at their mother's farm." It had made her sick to her stomach to remember that night and how she'd put Edward, Carmella and Alex in danger.

"But Alex took the tracker out, right? So why don't you want to use your coat?"

"I'm being paranoid. That's the new definition of 'cautious' these days."

Naomi's mouth twisted in a wry half smile at her quip, but Rachel knew she understood her tension. The entire Grant household had been stressed since Rachel had escaped the near-drowning two days ago.

"Let me get it for you." Naomi headed upstairs

to her room and Rachel followed. "Where are you going?"

"To the hospital."

"Why? Isn't Edward being discharged today?"

"I want to be there. Thanks." She took Naomi's coat from her. "Where's Dad? Alex is going to pick me up soon."

"Out in the garden, I think."

"It's kind of cold for him, isn't it?"

Naomi sent her a sidelong look. "He's been spending more time out there since you and he…fought and made up. And since the attempts on your life."

She hadn't talked to Dad much. She'd been too busy trying to play it safe, to see if there was anything else she could do to help Detective Carter find Lee or Gloria.

She supposed the good news was that her product launch was safe, now that Gloria was on the run. But the launch might still be delayed if she couldn't spend as much time at the lab as she needed to in order to get the clinical data analyzed and to start production.

Oh, and she had to hire a new research assistant, and this time, try not to pick someone who would stab her in the back.

And Edward was going home today, feeling good—according to him—and ready to take up his post as Rachel's personal bodyguard.

After all this was over, Rachel had hopes he'd continue to stick around.

She had reached the foot of the stairs and was about to turn toward the back of the house when her cell phone rang. It was Detective Carter. "Hello?"

"Hi, Rachel. We caught Lee."

"Thank God!" She sank onto the stairs, dropping the coat beside her, and rested her head in her hand. She could almost feel the acid in her stomach start to neutralize, relaxing her gut muscles from the stress of the past few days. "He's locked away? He won't get loose?"

"No. He won't get out on bail, and he seemed open to a full confession. It turns out Mr. Reynolds knew what his wife was doing, but didn't actively participate. However, he didn't try to stop her, either. We're pressing charges against him, too."

"And Gloria?"

"Still in the wind, but don't worry, Rachel, we'll get her. We also captured your lab assistant, Stephanie. She'd been holed up in one of the Sonoma farms."

Rachel had been worrying about that last thread. She didn't think Stephanie would try to harm her, but it hadn't made her feel very safe to know that she was out there, free.

"Everything will get back to normal soon," Detective Carter assured her.

Except Rachel didn't know if she really wanted everything exactly back to what her life had been like. Her eyes were more open to God, to her relationship with her father. And her heart was more open to a different type of relationship with Edward.

No, the way things used to be was gone. In this case, new would be a good thing.

A great thing.

"Thanks, Detective."

"Say hello to Edward for me today."

"I will." She said goodbye and closed her phone, just sitting on the stairs for a moment to let it sink in. Lee was in custody. He couldn't get to her. He was going to confess to everything.

She heard a footfall to her left, from the kitchen area. She peered through the open doorway. "Dad?"

No, that wouldn't be her father's wheelchair. But Naomi was upstairs. Monica and Aunt Becca had gone into Sonoma with Evita to pick up some supplies.

Her father's wheelchair came into view.

"Oh, there you are, Dad. I was just about to go looking—"

He was followed by Gloria Reynolds, holding a gun to his head.

Every nerve in Rachel's body zapped to life. She shot to her feet. "Gloria! Let him go."

The once-elegant spa client regarded her with smoldering eyes, full of wildfire, with dark bags under them. "You." She almost growled the word, her tone rich with loathing.

Her father's white face held a mixture of intense worry and also frustration that this crazed woman could so easily overtake him, that he couldn't fight her. "I'm sorry, Rachel. She made me undo the security alarm."

"Shut up." Gloria's normally prim hair was a halo about her head, and she tossed aside a heavy lock of it that had fallen in front of her eyes.

Rachel thought she caught a glimpse of movement behind Gloria, through the glass panels of the front door, but before she could look, Naomi's voice rang out in surprise from the landing on the second floor. "Gloria!"

"Stay back!" Gloria punctuated her words by jabbing the gun farther into her father's neck. He winced and swallowed.

"Let him go," Rachel said.

"It's all your fault," Gloria hissed, pushing her father into the foyer and taking a limping step forward on a broken pump heel.

"If you let him go, I'll come with you," Rachel said.

"Rach!" Naomi protested at the same time Dad shouted, "No!"

"You're not in a position to bargain," Gloria said.

"If you shoot me, or shoot him, Naomi can still call the police." She gestured to Naomi, looking over them all on the second-floor landing. "Alex is coming in a few minutes, too."

"You're just bluffing."

"I'm not. I'm offering you a way out. If I go with you right now, we can leave before Alex gets here.

You'll have more time to kill me, hide my body, run away."

"Rachel, what are you saying?" her father demanded.

"Just let my father go, and I'll come with you." Rachel held her hands out in front of her.

Gloria's lips were tight, but her face looked gaunt, with her eyes dark and huge. She shook her head, her hair falling in her eyes again. "I've lost everything, and it's all your fault. I just want you dead." She raised her gun at Rachel.

Edward yanked Alex to one side of the front door, out of sight. "Keep quiet," he whispered. Thank God he had decided to surprise Rachel by having Alex pick him up from the hospital early and then drive him to her house.

"What is it?" Alex whispered.

"I saw Gloria Reynolds in there with a gun." Pointed at Augustus Grant, with Rachel only a few yards away. It was the night in the parking lot all over again, and him unable to do anything.

Not this time.

He whipped out his cell phone. "Mama?"

"Edward, what—?" Her face stared at him from the truck window where it was parked in the Grants' driveway.

"Mama, just listen to me. Call Detective Carter right now. Gloria Reynolds is inside the Grant home. And stay in the truck!"

He shut his phone and motioned to Alex. "Follow me. We can enter through the back door." They darted around the corner of the house.

"What about the alarm?"

"They must have disarmed it or Gloria wouldn't be inside."

"Let's hope they didn't rearm it once she got in." Alex crouched down as they scuttled under the edge of a kitchen window. "And here we thought it would be *safer* to bring you to Rachel rather than driving her to the hospital."

"Horatio had just arrested Lee. Our plan *was* safer." Edward opened the wooden gate to the backyard slowly, praying the hinges wouldn't squeak. He slipped inside, followed by Alex, and then carefully closed the gate without a sound.

They crept along the side of the house and around the corner toward the back sliding glass door, which opened into the kitchen. If they were quiet enough, they could sneak up behind Gloria and Augustus.

That was a long distance to cover inside the house without making a sound.

"Let me do this." Alex nudged him aside and slowly slid open the glass door into the kitchen, just a mere inch.

No alarm.

Alex opened the door farther, trying to be both quick and quiet. If they didn't get in and close the door fast enough, Gloria might hear the outside sounds from the backyard and know the door was open.

Alex slithered inside, but Edward had to crack the door open a little more to be able to get his body through. As soon as his legs cleared the door, Alex again worked the sliding door in quiet inches until it was closed again.

Alex removed his shoes, and Edward followed suit. In their socks, they slid across the linoleum floor of the kitchen, able to see into the L-shaped breakfast area. The section closest to them was clear. They took slow steps inside, then peeked around the corner toward the open doorway into the foyer.

Gloria had already taken a few steps out of the breakfast area and stood within the foyer, her back to them. Edward couldn't see Rachel, but Gloria faced the base of the stairs, where he'd last seen her.

Gloria shook her head, her tangled hair falling in front of her eyes. "I've lost everything, and it's all your fault." Her voice was hoarse and trembling with rage. "I just want you dead."

She raised the gun.

For Edward, it was déjà vu, watching someone point a gun at Rachel, with him several feet away.

No. He'd just found her. He wouldn't lose her.

"Gloria!" he roared.

She swung the gun around toward him.

He didn't care—just as long as it wasn't pointing at Rachel.

Gloria reached up a hand to clear the hair that had fallen into her eyes.

Edward rushed her.

"No!" Augustus twisted in the chair and pushed at Gloria.

A flash of light. The explosion of the gun discharging.

A cannonball hit Edward in the left shoulder. He stumbled, but kept moving forward, his other hand swinging at the gun.

He collided with both her and Augustus in a cloud of acrid gunpowder. They all went down, the wheelchair clanking as it hit the foyer tiles.

Edward scrambled to grab Gloria, managing to pin one of her arms while she was still stunned by the fall.

A split second later she started to thrash violently, kicking at him. Augustus's face suddenly appeared across her body from him—he must have crawled from where he and his wheelchair fell. Augustus used his weight to pin her other arm, but the stroke had stolen the strength from his limbs, and he struggled to keep hold of Gloria.

She was crazed, and her mania gave her extraordinary strength. Alex tried to fall on her legs, but she kneed him in the chest, and he grunted as he fell back.

Then Naomi appeared, grabbing one leg while Alex grabbed the other, both of them bucking under Gloria's kicks.

"Rachel!" Augustus shouted. "Zip ties! Garage workbench—second drawer from the right!"

Running footsteps.

Gloria's back arched off the floor as she freed her arm from Augustus's weaker grip and whipped at Edward's head. The blow made him see stars for a moment, but he fought to keep his weight on her other wriggling arm.

He began to feel how the poison and the hospital stay had weakened him as his muscles trembled with fatigue. Where was Rachel with the zip ties?

Then Rachel was on her knees beside him, handing thin, stiff plastic ties to both him and Alex. His brother secured Gloria's legs first, then helped him flip her onto her stomach so they could tie her wrists.

Gloria screamed as she twisted and kicked against them. They forced her wrists together while Rachel strung a zip tie and pulled it tight.

Blood seamed where Gloria fought the bonds, but Naomi appeared with some kitchen twine, and she and Alex tied Gloria's feet to her wrists behind her back in a hog-tie.

Edward sat back, suddenly aware of the explosion of pain in his shoulder.

Rachel had run to get some kitchen towels which she now pressed to his shoulder. "Edward, hold still."

He grunted and squeezed his eyes shut as the pressure felt as if it would tear his arm out of the socket.

"We told Mama to call Horatio," Alex told them above Gloria's shrieking.

"Edward."

He felt Rachel's fingers on his cheek, his jaw, and he opened his eyes. Her face filled his vision, her bottom lip quivering.

"I'm fine," he gasped. And he was, now that she was safe.

The pain in his shoulder had dulled to a throbbing ache as she continued to apply pressure to it. Maybe it was the adrenaline rush, or maybe it was loss of blood, but the room began to spin.

"You saved my life." Her hand caressed his cheek.

He closed his eyes even as he smiled at her. "Give me a kiss and you'll save mine."

And then blackness.

TWENTY

The first thing Rachel saw when she entered Edward's hospital room was him about to bite into the largest chocolate-chip cookie she had ever seen. "Are you allowed to eat that? Is it even legal to have a cookie that big?"

Edward paused, the cookie inches from his mouth, and guilt painted his cheeks burgundy. Then he smiled at her, and the world tilted. "I wondered when you'd show up."

"Are you kidding?" Naomi entered the room behind her. "Rachel can sniff out a chocolate-chip cookie from fifty yards away."

"She's only scolding you because she wants to make sure she gets some of that," added her cousin Jane with a wink at Rachel as she wheeled Rachel's father into the room, followed by Monica.

"There's enough for everyone," Edward's mother said, breaking open a plastic container. "They're six-ounce cookies, Rachel, a copycat recipe of a famous New York bakery."

"Six ounces?" Her mouth watered.

"Save some for us," Aunt Becca said, cramming into the room with Detective Carter on her arm.

Rachel sidled up to Edward's hospital bed and took his hand. "How are you doing?"

His eyes crinkled at the corners. "As well as I was when you called an hour ago."

"You can't fault a girl for being worried when her man passes out in her arms."

"I didn't pass out," he protested. "I was just resting my eyes."

Her father wheeled to the side of the bed. "I'm glad you're doing well, young man."

Edward's eyes sobered as he held out his hand to him. "You saved my life. Thank you." The doctors had said that the bullet missed his heart by only a few inches.

Dad took Edward's hand. "God saved your life. And I want to thank you for doing what you did to save all of us."

"Don't feel too sorry for him," Alex said with a teasing grin. "He only got injured so he can leave me with all the work at the greenhouses."

"Alex!" His mother smacked his arm. "No cookies for you."

"Maybe I should apologize to Alex," Rachel said, leaning closer. Everyone around them was chatting, and she had pitched her voice low, but he could clearly hear her.

"Apologize? For what?"

She swallowed. "After all, I'm the reason you're

back in the hospital bed less than twelve hours after you were discharged."

"No, Rachel. None of this is your fault."

"When Gloria's gun went off, I couldn't move. I couldn't even scream. I was so afraid she had…" Her voice broke. She took a short breath, then continued, "And then I saw you wrestling with her, and I'd never been so relieved in my life, because you were alive."

All he saw was the pale oval of her face, close to him, her dark hazel eyes wide and intense.

"I love you, Edward."

Her words seemed to echo the words of a song that had been playing in Edward's head, in his heart, for months. A song he'd tried to drown out, to ignore. A song that resonated with Rachel's laugh, with the sparkle in her eyes, with the quickness of her humor and, more recently, with the fire in her spirit.

"You don't have to say anything," she hastened to assure him. "I just…I just wanted you to know."

He couldn't say anything. He was too…full. He took her hand in his and kissed her knuckles, her skin silky soft against his lips.

"I think I've loved you for a long time. Maybe since the moment we shook hands, when I had decided to hire you to grow my Malaysian basil plants." She smiled suddenly. "How unromantic. Love over a basil plant."

"The smell of basil always reminds me of you." The

words spilled from his mouth and made him want to kick himself at how stupid they sounded.

But Rachel laughed, her joy a bright flame he couldn't help but be drawn toward.

"I've been fighting my feelings for a long time, Rach. I've misjudged you, I've abandoned you, I've done everything that should have made you stop loving me."

She shook her head. "You've saved my life. Several times."

"Today, seeing Gloria point that gun at you, feeling helpless and unable to do anything to stop her—that sealed it for me. It made me realize what I want, what I need, what God has given to me."

Her lips parted as she stared at him. "Edward…"

"I want you to know that this is coming from the bottom of my heart, that it's not something I'm just saying. I love you."

There was a heartbeat where all the noise in the room faded away, and her gaze was as intimate as a kiss.

He picked up her right hand, fingering the ruby ring that had saved her life. "I have a ring at home, turquoise in silver. It belonged to my grandmother, and I want you to wear it. On your left hand."

She looked as if she'd stopped breathing for a moment. "Are you sure?"

"I'm more sure of that than anything else in my life right now. I love you, and I'm serious about my feelings for you. If you're not ready right now, that's fine, but I wanted to let you know."

She gripped his fingers and smiled into his eyes. "Oh, Edward. I feel like I'm going to burst."

"And after everything that has happened lately, I'm not wasting any more time," he said.

He reached out, cupped her head tenderly and drew her in for a kiss amidst a shower of cheers and laughter.

* * * * *

Dear Reader,

Thank you for joining me on this fun trip through the gorgeous agricultural county of Sonoma, California! This tourist spot still has all the charm of a small farming community, where neighbors help each other and romance abounds among the scenic rolling foothills.

Rachel's story is very close to my heart because I'm also a geek who struggles with shyness and awkward social skills. I'm not as brilliant as Rachel is (unfortunately!), but her need to understand how much her heavenly Father loves her is something I can relate to and still struggle with in my own life.

Rachel's theme Bible verse reminds me that God is always in control of everything, and He is everything I will ever need. It was a bit cathartic to write that same realization for Rachel, since I have to keep reminding myself of that fact all the time. But God is full of patience as well as love!

I love to hear from readers! You can e-mail me at camy@camytang.com or write to me at P.O. Box 23143, San Jose, CA 95123-3143. I blog about knitting, my dog, knitting, tea, knitting, my husband's coffee fixation, knitting, food—oh, and did I mention my knitting obsession?—at camys-loft.blogspot.com/. I hope to see you all there.

Camy
Tang

QUESTIONS FOR DISCUSSION

1. Rachel is a dermatologist researcher who creates products exclusively used at the Joy Luck Life spa for their high-end clients. Her newest launch is in only five months, which puts a lot of time pressure on her. She doesn't deal with pressure very well, it seems. How about you? How do you respond under time pressure at home or work? What do you know you should do in those situations?"

2. Edward's greenhouse is broken into, and Rachel's plants are in danger of being destroyed, setting back months of work he's put into cultivating the basil. How does he deal with the situation? Is there anything he should do differently? How would you feel if your work was sabotaged this way?

3. Edward's brother, Alex, is a strong Christian who is comfortable speaking about his faith. Can you relate to him or do you know someone like him? What is your own way of sharing your faith?

4. Rachel and her cousin Jane are close friends, partly because of the accident Rachel caused when they were young girls, but also partly because they're very similar—both are geeky

and shy. Are you close with any of your cousins or family members? Is there someone you might want to make an effort to get closer to?

5. When Rachel realizes someone is after her research, she feels helpless, violated and stressed. Have you been in a situation where things were completely out of your control and it seemed to be going from bad to worse? How did you feel? What did you do?

6. Although Rachel has been a Christian since she was young, she feels as if she's just going through the motions and that God doesn't hear her prayers. Can you relate to how she's feeling? What should she do?

7. Rachel has a poor relationship with her father, and Edward's warm family circle draws her in. Why is it important to have people—either family or like family—around you? Do you have a "family" circle of your own?

8. As things get worse, Rachel knows she needs to trust God and believe that He has everything under His control, but she has a hard time doing this. Instead, she takes charge, attempting to do something about the people trying to steal her research and kill her. Have you ever felt this way? How did you respond? What would you have done differently from Rachel?

9. Rachel wants to trust her research assistant, Stephanie, but at the same time doesn't know if she can (and, as it ends up, Stephanie isn't as innocent as she seems). Have you ever been in a situation where you didn't know if you could extend trust to someone? What did you do? Many times it depends on the stakes involved (for Rachel, the stakes were her research and her life). What were the stakes involved in your own situation?

10. Edward is still struggling with the hurt his workaholic father inflicted on him and his family, and he initially sees Rachel as being the same type of work-focused person. Do you know someone for whom their work has become their "God"? What can or should we as Christians do for them?

11. Rachel's father treats her differently than he does his other daughters because he doesn't understand her very well. Rachel was simply internalizing his criticism and letting it damage her self-esteem. Can you relate to how she was feeling? Do you worry that you might be doing that to someone else? What can we do?

12. Rachel's theme verse is Psalm 24:1: "The earth is the Lord's, and everything in it, the world, and all who live in it." What does that verse mean for you?

LARGER-PRINT BOOKS!

GET 2 FREE
LARGER-PRINT NOVELS
PLUS 2 FREE
MYSTERY GIFTS

Love Inspired®
SUSPENSE
RIVETING INSPIRATIONAL ROMANCE

Larger-print novels are now available...

YES! Please send me 2 FREE LARGER-PRINT Love Inspired® Suspense novels and my 2 FREE mystery gifts (gifts are worth about $10). After receiving them, if I don't wish to receive any more books, I can return the shipping statement marked "cancel". If I don't cancel, I will receive 4 brand-new novels every month and be billed just $4.74 per book in the U.S. or $5.24 per book in Canada. That's a saving of over 20% off the cover price. It's quite a bargain! Shipping and handling is just 50¢ per book.* I understand that accepting the 2 free books and gifts places me under no obligation to buy anything. I can always return a shipment and cancel at any time. Even if I never buy another book, the two free books and gifts are mine to keep forever.

110/310 IDN E7RD

Name	(PLEASE PRINT)

Address	Apt. #

City	State/Prov.	Zip/Postal Code

Signature (if under 18, a parent or guardian must sign)

Mail to Steeple Hill Reader Service:
IN U.S.A.: P.O. Box 1867, Buffalo, NY 14240-1867
IN CANADA: P.O. Box 609, Fort Erie, Ontario L2A 5X3

Not valid for current subscribers to Love Inspired Suspense larger-print books.

**Are you a current subscriber to Love Inspired Suspense books
and want to receive the larger-print edition?
Call 1-800-873-8635 or visit www.morefreebooks.com.**

* Terms and prices subject to change without notice. Prices do not include applicable taxes. Sales tax applicable in N.Y. Canadian residents will be charged applicable provincial taxes and GST. Offer not valid in Quebec. This offer is limited to one order per household. All orders subject to approval. Credit or debit balances in a customer's account(s) may be offset by any other outstanding balance owed by or to the customer. Please allow 4 to 6 weeks for delivery. Offer available while quantities last.

LISUSLP10R